NEW

MOUNTAINS

FORT EDWARD

FORT Wᵐ. HENRY

HUDSON RIVER

The Last
of the Mohicans

◇◇◇◇◇◇◇◇◇◇◇◇◇◇◇◇◇◇◇◇◇◇◇◇◇◇◇◇◇◇◇◇◇◇◇◇

Written by James Fenimore Cooper,
an American author who lived from
1789 to 1851—an adventure story of
war between the English and French,
when Indian war whoops echoed
through the deep forests of the New
World. Here are many thrills—fights
between Indians, rescues of beautiful
girls held prisoner, hairbreadth es-
capes, and a bloody massacre.

BY JAMES FENIMORE COOPER

ILLUSTRATED BY Brinton Turkle

The Last
of the Mohicans

ADAPTED BY

Verne B. Brown *and edited by*
Gertrude Moderow

Scott, Foresman and Company

Chicago   Atlanta   Dallas   New York

Contents

PART ONE **A journey through Indian country**

PART TWO **A wild flight through enemy lines**

◆◇

PART THREE **The massacre
at Fort William Henry**

PART FOUR **In the camp
of the enemy**

◇◇

PART FIVE **War between
the Hurons and Delawares**

◇◇

A journey through Indian country

CHAPTER 1

Bloody Ground

◇◇◇

IT WAS near the end of a summer day when an Indian runner [1] appeared at Fort Edward with news that frightened everyone there. Montcalm, the French general from Canada, had been seen on Lake Champlain with an army, "as many as the leaves on the trees"—with flags flying, bands playing, soldiers in full dress, and Indians in canoes—thousands of them.

This was during the French and Indian War, when both France and England were struggling for control of the New World. As the English believed, Montcalm planned to go through Lake Champlain and Lake George, where he would attack Fort William Henry.

[1] *runner*, one who runs errands. The Indian runners were very swift.

◇◇

From there he hoped to march south, take Fort Edward on the Hudson River, and gain control of much of the land held by the English.

Colonel Munro, who was in command at Fort William Henry, had with him a force far too small to hold his fort against Montcalm. He urged General Webb, who was in command at Fort Edward, to send him men at once.

Colonel Munro's two daughters were then at Fort Edward on their way to visit their father, and Munro had sent one of his young officers, Major Duncan Heyward, to accompany them. They had already prepared for the trip when Munro's message came.

General Webb spoke to Major Heyward:

"Tomorrow you will return to Fort William Henry?" he asked.

"Colonel Munro will need me now more than ever, sir," said Heyward. "And he will need some of the King's soldiers that you have here. Montcalm is an able leader."

"An able leader, yes," said Webb, "but he is a long way from his supplies. I'll send fifteen hundred men in the morning. Will you return with them?"

"Yes, sir," replied Major Heyward. "This Indian

runner knows a secret path by which he came from Fort William Henry today, and he offers to lead us back." Then he added, almost to himself, "Only fifteen hundred men—even then you will have twice as many as Munro."

"That is all I can spare," said Webb, shortly. "We must hold Fort Edward."

"I hope, sir," said Major Heyward quietly, "that before it is too late, you will see how Munro needs your help."

News soon spread that some of Edward's men would leave at dawn for William Henry. Preparations began at once. The young soldiers hurried about with worried faces. Even the most skilled men showed no liking for this fighting in the wilderness, but by night all was ready.

Early the next morning the heavy sleep of the army was broken by the roll of drums. In a moment the whole camp was awake and soon the chosen troops were in position to start. Scouts set out ahead. Next came heavy wagons loaded with supplies. They rolled noisily over the rough road through the woods, with strong guards before and behind them. And before the sun was fairly up, the main body of fighting men wheeled into col-

umn.² To the right marched the trained, proud, red-coated ³ soldiers of the King. To the left, the humble provincials ⁴ lined up. To the music of fife and drum, and with flags flying, they marched away until the forest seemed to swallow the line.

Many of the men who remained behind had watched their friends as they marched away. Then they turned toward another interesting scene. Out of the General's headquarters came the boyish-looking Major Heyward with the two young women. The younger girl had bright blue eyes, golden hair, and a smile as cheering as the morning itself. The other, who looked four or five years older than her sister, had hair as black as night, dark eyes, rich color in her cheeks, and delicate features that made her beautiful indeed. Both were dressed for the difficult ride in the woods.

---

² *wheeled into column.* They took their places, one behind the other, for the march along the narrow road through the forest.

³ *red-coated.* The soldiers of the regular army, those sent over from England, wore handsome uniforms, which included red coats.

⁴ *provincials,* soldiers from the provinces, or colonies. They were not so well trained and not so well fitted out as the soldiers of the regular army.

The officer helped the girls to mount horses that were waiting, then sprang lightly upon his own horse. All three bowed to General Webb, who stood at the door of his cabin, then turned and followed the soldiers.

Suddenly the Indian runner crossed their path and stepped out in front to lead the way. A little cry of alarm escaped the younger of the girls. The older made no sound, but over her face there came a look of both admiration and horror as she watched the easy motion of the savage. Then she smiled as if at her own fear and rode on in silence.

CHAPTER 2

The Secret Journey

◇◇◇

WHILE the older of the two girls was lost in thought, the younger also recovered from her fear at the Indian's sudden appearance. Laughing, she asked of the officer at her side:

"Is this a spirit of the woods, Major Heyward? Or did you order this sight to entertain us? If it is a spirit, Cora and I shall have to remember that we come from a family famous for its bravery. And we shall have to begin using that bravery even before we meet Montcalm."

"This Indian is a runner of the army," replied the officer. "He has offered to guide us to Lake George by a secret path. He says that will be quicker, since the road is blocked by our own soldiers."

"I don't like him," said Alice, turning away. "But you know him, don't you? Or you would not trust yourself to his keeping."

"I might trust myself, but certainly not you and your sister," he replied. "With you in my care, I would take no chance with a guide who was not honest. This man is a Canadian, but he has served with the Mohawks, who are one of the Six Nations." [1]

"But if he has been my father's enemy," said Alice, "I like him still less!"

"True. This Indian was brought to us by some strange misdeed with which your father had to deal," explained the officer. "He was severely punished at the time, but he is our friend now. Your father trusted him—even with the news of the coming of the French army under General Montcalm."

[1] *Six Nations*, a very strong union of six tribes: Mohawks, Oneidas, Onondagas, Cayugas, Senecas, and Tuscaroras. The French name for the Six Nations was *Iroquois*.

The Indian stopped, then pointed to a path that led into the thickest part of the woods—a path wide enough for only one horse at a time.

"Would we not be safer if we journey with the soldiers?" asked Alice.

"Not knowing the ways of the Indians, you would not know the place of greatest danger," said Heyward. "If there are enemies near, they will follow the troops, where many scalps can be taken. They know the route of the soldiers; this is a secret path."

At this moment Cora spoke. "Shall we fear the man because his manners are different from ours and because his skin is dark?" she asked coldly.

This was enough to win Alice. Giving her horse a smart cut with the whip, she was the first to push aside the branches and follow the runner along the dark, wooded path into which he now led them. Cora's courage and the ease with which she won her sister delighted the officer. He even let Alice, the younger though certainly not more beautiful sister, go a little way alone while he opened the path for the older girl.

As they plunged "Indian file" [2] into the forest, all was quiet. But suddenly horses' hoofs could be heard in the path behind them. There could be no mistake. They were being followed. The whole party stopped quickly.

In a few minutes a colt appeared, running like a deer among the straight pine trees. Soon there followed a horse and on it a bony stranger who had admired Heyward's horse in front of the General's cabin earlier in the day, although Heyward and the girls had not seen him at that time.

A strange sight he had been on foot, but on horseback he was really surprising. In spite of his efforts with a spur, he could not put his horse to more than a gallop, but most of the time she mixed the gallop with a trot. As the man rode along, he rose in the stirrups to a great height, then sank far down. Not only this, but since the spur was used on only one side of the horse, that side seemed to go faster than the other.

Heyward was quietly amused, Alice smiled openly, and even the dark eyes of Cora lighted with fun.

[2] *Indian file*, single file, one behind the other.

◇◇

"Do you bring us news?" asked Heyward.

The man fanned himself a moment before he spoke. "I heard you were riding to William Henry and, as I am going there myself, I thought we might keep each other company."

"You have taken the wrong way," said Heyward coldly. "The road is at least a half mile behind you."

"True," returned the man, paying no attention to this poor welcome. "I've been at Fort Edward a week and I'd be dumb not to know the road. And if I were dumb I'd find it hard to do my work." He gave a silly laugh as if he had said something funny and was laughing at his own joke. "Anyway, I don't want to be too close to the troops. A gentleman like you knows best about travel, so I have decided to join you for a friendly journey."

"So you have decided, have you?" asked Heyward, growing angry but still wanting to laugh at the stranger. "And what is this work you speak of?"

"I hope I don't offend you," said the man, "but I claim a little skill in the art of praying and giving thanks. I am a singer of psalms."

"Let him come along," cried Alice, laughing. "Come, Duncan, look pleasant! I want to hear some of his songs." Then she looked at Cora, who was following the sour-looking but quiet guide, and her face became serious. "He may be a friend in need," she added in a low voice, "and we may need strength."

Hurt by her words, Major Heyward spoke quickly:

"Do you think, Alice, that I would trust those I love to this guide if I thought there was any danger?"

Alice's face lighted up again. "Oh, let's not even think of it. I'm sure everything is all right. But this strange man amuses me. If he has music in his soul, let's be nice to him." She looked up eagerly at Heyward, who smiled and nodded. Then he spurred his horse and in a few bounds was at the side of Cora.

"Friend," said Alice to the stranger, "I like to sing myself. We'll all try a song. It might be good for the rest of us to hear the opinion of a teacher of music."

"Man's voice," said the stranger, "like his other powers, is given to him for use. I am glad that, as a boy, I learned music as did the royal David—holy music. I have sung the songs of David and the songs of the New Testament."

He fitted a pair of iron-rimmed spectacles to his nose. He took from his pocket a book and a pitch pipe. Then,

◇◇◇

taking his key from the pipe, he began to sing. His voice, although soft and sweet, could be heard easily by those on the path ahead. The Indian spoke a few words in broken English to Heyward, who spoke to the singer.

"Although we are not in danger, it would be wise to travel through the forest as quietly as possible. You will pardon me, Alice, if I ask this gentleman not to sing until we are in a safer place."

"Oh, what a pity," cried Alice. "I was going to learn all about psalms and singing."

"The safety of you and Cora means more to me than the finest music," replied Heyward.

He stopped talking and glanced quickly at the bushes, and then at the guide who was going on ahead. Then he smiled at his own fears. He told himself that what he thought was the fierce eye of a hidden savage must have been some shining berry. So he rode on, continuing to talk to the two girls.

The party had not gone far, however, before a face as fierce as savage art and hate could make it peered out from the bushes at the disappearing travelers. A look of joy shot across the face of the Indian as he looked at his innocent prey—the two girls, Heyward's manly figure, and the shapeless person of the singer. But not knowing their danger, they rode on until hidden by the many trunks of the mighty trees.

CHAPTER 3

The Redskin's [1] Story

◇◇

AT THE very hour when Major Duncan Heyward and his companions were traveling deeper and deeper into danger, two men were sitting on the banks of a small but rapid stream, within an hour's journey of Fort Edward. Though the rushing water cooled the hot air, there was still a sleepy warmth over this hidden spot. The only sounds to break the stillness were the voices of the two men, the lazy call of a bird, or the whisper of a waterfall.

One of these men was an Indian, with Indian dress and weapons. The other, though deeply sunburned, was a white man—a "paleface." The Indian was sitting on

[1] *redskin,* an Indian—often called this because of the copper color of his skin.

the end of a fallen log, calmly motioning in the manner
of his people as he talked. On his naked body was
painted, in black and white, a sign of death. The hair
had been cut from his head except for his scalp lock.[2] An
eagle feather, tied in this lock, hung over the top of his
head and his left shoulder. In his belt were a tomahawk [3]
and a long knife of English make. Across his bare knees
lay a short rifle such as the whites furnished the Indians.
He seemed well past middle age, with broad chest, well-
formed limbs, and the proud look of a warrior.

The white man's build showed that he too had lived
much of his life out of doors and had known hard work.
His hunting shirt was forest green, trimmed with yellow. His cap was made of skins of animals. In his belt he
carried a knife, but no tomahawk. On his feet were moccasins, and below the long skirt of his coat was a pair of
deerskin leggings. He carried a pouch and powder horn
for his long-barreled rifle that was now leaning against a
tree. His quick eye darted about as if on guard always
against an enemy. In the language of the Indians of
that country, he spoke:

----

[2] *scalp lock*, lock of hair on the top of the head of some American Indians. This
lock was taken with the scalp when an enemy was killed.

[3] *tomahawk*, an Indian ax of stone or metal.

◇◇◇

"As for me, I cannot see that the white man is so wicked. True enough, he may have taken your hunting grounds. But didn't he follow the Indian's example? Your fathers came from the direction of the setting sun, crossed the big river, fought the people of this country, and took their land. My fathers came from the red sky of the morning, over the salt sea, and took the land you had taken from others. Why not let God decide who was wrong and who was right, and let friends talk of other things?"

"My fathers fought a fair fight with naked red men like themselves," returned the Indian sternly. "Is there no difference, Hawkeye, between the stone-headed arrow of the Indian and the lead bullet with which you kill?"

Hawkeye was silent. At first he could find no answer to the red man's question but, after a moment's thought, he replied as well as he could:

"A rifle against a bow and arrow may seem like an unfair fight. But, judging from what I have seen at deer and squirrel hunts, I should think that a rifle was not so dangerous as a good flint head [4] might be if drawn with Indian judgment and guided by an Indian eye. Still,

---

[4] *flint head,* hard stone sharpened to form the head of an arrow.

every story has its two sides. So I ask you, Great Serpent,[5] what do the Indians tell of those early times when our fathers first met?"

After a short silence, the Indian began his story.

"My fathers came from out there where the sun hides himself each night, over great plains where the buffaloes live, until they reached the big river. There they fought the river tribes till the ground was red with their blood. Then they crossed the river and came on to the salt sea. They took the land like warriors; they held it like men. They drew fish from the lakes; they hunted in the forests."

"All this I have heard before, and I believe it," said Hawkeye, "but this happened long before the white men came into the country."

"The palefaces came into our land where we were living at peace with the other red men. We were one people and we were happy," the Indian continued with deep feeling. "We worshiped the Great Spirit. The salt sea gave us its fish, the wood its deer, and the air its birds."

"I suppose your own family must have been brave warriors and wise men at the council fire."

---

[5] *Great Serpent.* Hawkeye's friend had received this name because he was a wise man and because the serpent, or snake, used to be considered very sly and cunning.

◇◇

"My tribe is the grandfather of nations," [6] said the Indian proudly. "The blood of chiefs flows in me. The palefaces came and gave my people firewater.[7] They drank until the heavens and the earth seemed to meet. They thought they had found the Great Spirit. Then my people traded away their land. Foot by foot they were driven back from the shores. And I, a chief, have never seen the sun shine except through the trees, and have never visited the graves of my fathers."

"But where are your race who came to the Delaware country so many summers ago?"

"All my family have gone to the land of spirits— fallen one by one," said Great Serpent sadly. "I am on the top of the hill and must soon go down into the valley. And when Uncas, my son, follows me, there will no longer be any of the blood of my family, for Uncas is the last of the Mohicans."

"Uncas is here," said a soft, low voice from the bushes. "Who speaks to Uncas?"

Hawkeye had reached quickly for his gun, but the

[6] *grandfather of nations.* The Mohican tribe belonged to the larger group of Delawares. Before the coming of the white men, the Delawares had come from farther west and taken the land around Delaware Bay and the Delaware River, forcing other Indians out. They proudly thought of themselves as the "grandfather of nations."

[7] *firewater,* Indian word for strong drink.

Indian showed no surprise. The next moment a young warrior silently stepped in between them and seated himself on the bank of the stream. The white man laid his gun aside and sat quietly while the Great Serpent turned his eyes toward his son.

"Do the Hurons [8] dare to leave the print of their moccasins in these woods?" he asked.

"I have been on their trail," replied the young Indian. "They number as many as the fingers of my two hands, but they lie hid as if afraid."

"The thieves are after scalps or anything they can lay their hands on," said Hawkeye. "That busy Frenchman, Montcalm, will send his spies into our very camp, but he will find out what road we travel!"

"Hawkeye, tonight let us eat," said Great Serpent boldly, "and tomorrow show the Hurons that we are men."

"I am ready," said the scout. "But to fight the Hu-

[8] *Hurons,* Indians from farther north. The Hurons were friends of the French.

rons, we must find them; and to eat, we must get game."
His eyes looked carefully into the distance. "There in
the bushes below the hill is the biggest pair of antlers
I've seen this season. Now, Uncas," he laughed, "I'll
bet you my horn three times full of powder against a
foot of wampum,[9] that I can take him between the
eyes, and nearer to the right than to the left."

"That cannot be," cried the young Indian, springing
eagerly to his feet. "All but the tips of the horns are
hid."

"He's just a boy," laughed the white man. "Does he
think that when a hunter sees a part of a deer, he can't
tell where the rest of it ought to be?"

Hawkeye raised his gun, but the older Indian struck
it with his hand.

"Hawkeye, if you shoot, Hurons hear."

"Then I must leave the deer to your arrow, Uncas,"
said Hawkeye, for he knew that Great Serpent was
right.

The father motioned to Uncas, who threw himself on
the ground and crept quietly toward the animal. When
he was within a few yards of it, he carefully fitted an ar-

---

[9] *wampum*, beads made of shells. They were used as money, as ornaments, and
as badges of honor.

row to his bow. The snap of the string was heard, a white flash was seen, and the deer plunged to the very feet of its enemy.

"True Indian skill!" said the scout. "And it was a pretty sight to see. But, by the Lord, there must be a drove of them, and if they come within range of my gun, I'll drop one, though the whole Six Nations should hear."

Great Serpent put his ear close to the ground. "There is only one deer, and he is dead, but I hear the sound of feet!" He returned to his seat on the log. "The horses of white men are coming. Hawkeye, they are your brothers. Speak to them."

"That will I," said the scout, "but I see nothing, nor do I hear the sound of man or beast. Strange that an Indian should understand better than a white man the sounds that are made by a white man. But now I see the bushes move—and here they are. God save them from the Hurons!"

CHAPTER 4

Lost in the Deep Forest

◇◇◇

THE WORDS of the scout were hardly spoken when the leader of the party came into view.

"Who comes?" demanded Hawkeye, throwing his rifle over his left arm, his finger on the trigger.

"Believers in religion, and friends to the King," replied the singer, who was in the lead. "We have journeyed since sunrise, and we are tired and hungry. Can you tell us how far it is to Fort William Henry?"

"William Henry, man!" laughed Hawkeye. "If you are friends to the King and have business with the army, you had better go back to Fort Edward and speak to General Webb."

"How far are we from Fort Edward?" asked Major

Heyward, who had now come forward. "We left there this morning to travel to the head of the lake."

"Now what could be wrong with the road through the woods?" asked Hawkeye.

"It is a good road, I know," answered Heyward. "We trusted an Indian guide to take us by a nearer secret path, but we are lost."

"An Indian lost in the woods!" said the scout, shaking his head in doubt. "An Indian lost—with the sun up? with the streams running full? when the moss on every beech tree will tell [1] him from what direction the north star will shine at night? Is he a Mohawk?"

"Not by birth, but he has been adopted by them. He was born farther north—a Huron, I think."

"Hugh!" [2] exclaimed Great Serpent and Uncas, as they sprang to their feet in surprise.

"A Huron!" repeated Hawkeye, again shaking his head. "They are a thieving race, and you can never trust them."

"But our guide is a Mohawk now, and serves our forces as a friend."

---

[1] *moss . . . will tell.* When moss is found on the trunk of a tree, one can usually tell which is the north side of the tree. The north side gets no sun, is more damp, and so has more moss than the other sides.

[2] *Hugh.* With this grunt they were expressing both surprise and scorn.

◇◇

"He who is born a Huron will die a Huron," returned
Hawkeye. "Give me a Delaware, especially a Mohican,
for honesty. And when they will fight—which some of
them won't do—look to a Delaware—or a Mohican—
for a warrior."

"Enough," said Heyward, losing his patience. "You
know nothing about my guide, and you have not answered my question. If you will tell me the distance to
Fort Edward, and guide us there, I'll pay you well."

"Guide you to the army?" cried Hawkeye. "You may
be a spy for Montcalm. Not every man who speaks English is an honest subject."

"If you are with the English troops, you must know
of the regiment ³ of the King called the Sixtieth?" said
Heyward.

"I wear a hunting shirt instead of a red jacket," said
Hawkeye, "but you can tell me little of the Royal Americans ⁴ that I don't already know."

"Then do you know the name of the major who com-
mands the companies of regulars ⁵ at William Henry?"

"Yes, yes, I have heard of a young gentleman of
wealth from one of the southern provinces. He is very

³ *regiment*, a part of an army commanded by a colonel.
⁴ *Royal Americans*, the Sixtieth regiment. They were from Virginia.
⁵ *regulars*, men of the regular army.

◇◇

young to hold such rank, and yet they say he is a good soldier and a brave gentleman."

"However he may be fitted for his rank, it is he who now speaks to you, and he can be no enemy," said Heyward.

Hawkeye lifted his cap in surprise and respect, and, although still somewhat in doubt, he asked:

"Is this the party that was to leave the camp this morning for the lake shore?"

"That is right. But I wanted to take a nearer route, and I trusted my Indian guide."

"And he deceived you and then deserted?"

"I do not believe he deceived me, although I must say I began to doubt him and sent him to the rear," said Heyward. "You will find him there now."

"I want to look at him. I can tell a real Huron by his looks and by his paint," said Hawkeye. Peering through the bushes, he saw the runner leaning against a maple tree with a look on his face that was dark and savage. He returned to Heyward.

"A Mingo [6] is a Mingo, and neither the Mohawks nor any other tribe can change him. If we were alone, I

[6] *Mingo*, the Delaware term of scorn for an enemy, especially the Hurons.

◇◇◇

could return you to Fort Edward in an hour, but with ladies in the party it is impossible."

"Why?" asked Heyward. "They are tired, but they can ride a few miles more."

"No," said Hawkeye. "Night is coming and I wouldn't go a mile in these woods after dark for the best rifle in the colonies. They are full of Hurons and your false guide knows too well where to find them."

"You think so?"

"There he is leaning against that sugar maple. From where I stand I can take him between the foot and the knee, and he won't run again for a month," said Hawkeye as he stroked his gun.

"I do not like that," said Heyward, "although I feel sure now that he has tricked us."

"You can always count on the trickery of the Hurons," said Hawkeye.

He called his two Indian companions to him, and in low tones they all spoke seriously in the Delaware language. Then Uncas and his father laid down their weapons and, taking opposite sides of the path, moved carefully into the bushes.

"Now, you go back and hold the devil in talk," said

◇◇◇

Hawkeye to Heyward. "These two Mohicans here will take him without even breaking his paint."

"No," said the Major proudly, "I'll take him myself."

"What could you do, mounted, against an Indian in the bushes?"

"I will get off my horse."

"The moment he sees one of your feet out of the stirrup, he will escape. When you deal with natives, you must use native methods. Go and talk to him as if you were his best friend."

Although Heyward did not like the plan, he knew that the safety of his party depended upon quick action. The sun was low. He knew it was near the hour which the savages usually choose for their most cruel acts. As he passed the sisters, he spoke a few words to encourage them. Then, putting the spurs to his horse, he was soon near the false guide, who stood leaning against the maple tree.

"You see that the night is closing around us." Heyward tried to speak in a free and easy manner. "We are far from Fort William Henry. We have missed our way. But here is a hunter—the man you hear talking to the singer. He knows the deer paths and will lead us to a safe place for the night."

◇◇

"Then Sly Fox will go and the palefaces will see none but their own color."

"Who is Sly Fox?"

"That is the name my Canadian fathers gave to me. Night is the same as day to Sly Fox when Munro waits for him."

"And will Sly Fox dare to tell Munro that his two daughters are without a guide when Sly Fox promised to be one?"

"Sly Fox will go to the woods. He will not hear Munro."

"But what will the Mohawks say? They will make him a woman's skirt and keep him in the wigwam with the squaws."

"Sly Fox knows the way to the great lakes. He can find the graves of his fathers," answered the runner.

"But are we not friends?" asked Heyward. "Munro has promised you a gift for helping us and I shall give you another. Open your wallet [7] and eat, for we have only a few moments. When the ladies are rested we shall go on."

"It is good," spoke the Indian. Then, turning away, he sat down to eat food from his wallet.

[7] *wallet,* a bag. At that time it was used to carry food and supplies for a journey.

"This is well," said Heyward; "and Sly Fox will have strength and sight to find the path in the morning." He paused, for sounds like the snapping of a dry twig, and the rustling of leaves came from the nearby bushes. "We must be moving before the sun is seen, or Montcalm may find us and shut us out from the fort."

Sly Fox's hand dropped to his side, and though his eyes were fastened on the ground, his head was turned so that he could catch any sound. There he sat still as a statue, but his eyes and ears were awake. While Heyward waited, Sly Fox raised himself to his feet with a slow and guarded motion that made not the slightest noise. Heyward knew that he must act now. Swinging his right leg over the saddle, he got off his horse, hoping to catch the runner. But to prevent Sly Fox from becoming alarmed, he still acted calm and friendly.

"Sly Fox does not eat," said the Major. "His corn seems dry. Let me see if I can find something better."

The Indian held out his wallet and even let Heyward's hand touch his, but when he felt the hand moving gently along his arm, he struck it aside. Then he gave a sharp cry and, with a single bound, threw himself into the forest. At the next moment the form of

Great Serpent appeared from the bushes and slipped across the path after him. Next came a shout from Uncas, and then the woods were lighted by a quick flash, followed by the report of the hunter's rifle.

CHAPTER 5

A Secret Hiding Place

◇◇

THE SUDDEN escape of Sly Fox and the wild cries of the others so surprised Heyward that he stood staring after them for a moment. Then he dashed aside the bushes and ran after them, but soon he met them returning.

"Didn't you find him?" he exclaimed. "He must be hiding behind some of these trees. We are not safe with him loose."

"Would you set a cloud to chase the wind?" returned the scout. "I heard him brushing over the dry twigs, like a black snake, and I pulled on him, but my aim was too quick. Ha, look at this sumac![1] It is red, though everyone knows the blossom is yellow in July."

---

[1] *sumac*, a bush or small tree. Its leaves and bark are used in tanning.

◇◇

"It's blood! You hit him!"

"I cut the bark on him," laughed the scout, "but it only made him leap the farther."

"We are four able bodies against one wounded man," said Heyward.

"That red devil would soon draw us within reach of the tomahawks of his Indian friends," said Hawkeye. "I've often slept with the war whoop [2] ringing in my ears, and I should have known better than to fire this gun. Come, friends, we must move so as to throw that Mingo off our trail, or our scalps will be drying in the wind tomorrow."

As his eyes looked into the gathering darkness of the forest, Heyward imagined he saw the ugly faces of his enemies peering from their hiding places.

"Stay with me," he begged of the three. "Help me to protect those in my care, and you may name your own reward."

The two Indians and Hawkeye talked together in low voices in the Indian language. Heyward knew they were considering some plan for the good of the travelers, and again he tried to make them understand that he would pay whatever they might ask.

[2] *war whoop*, the Indian cry or call to battle.

Hawkeye spoke in English:

"Uncas is right. It would not be human to leave these women to their fate, even though it breaks up our secret hiding place forever. If you want to save them——"

"I have offered to pay you."

"Offer your prayers," said Hawkeye quietly, "but spare your offers of money, for you may not live to pay it or I to receive it. These Mohicans and I will do what we can to keep your party from harm. We want no pay, but both you and your friends must promise two things."

"Name them."

"One is that, whatever happens, you will be as still as the sleeping woods. The other is that you will never tell to a living soul the place to which we shall take you."

"I will do everything I can to keep both promises," said Heyward.

"Then follow, for we are losing valuable time."

Alice and Cora received the news with secret terror, but they got off their horses and went quickly and quietly to the water's edge, where Hawkeye, with silent motions of his arms, was calling the party together.

"What shall we do with these horses?" he asked. "To leave them here would be to tell these Mingoes that their owners are near."

◇◇◇

"Leave them free and let them range," said Heyward.

Just then Hawkeye heard a stir in the bushes and saw the colt. "That colt, at least, must die," he said. "Uncas, your arrows."

As Uncas let his arrows go, the wounded colt reared on its hind legs and fell forward on its knees. The Great Serpent quickly passed his knife across its throat and threw its body into the river, where it floated down the stream and away. The act seemed cruel, but it warned the party of their danger. The sisters stood with their arms around each other, while Heyward drew one of his pistols and placed himself in front of the girls.

The Indians led the horses into the bed of the river, moved upstream, and soon were hidden under the steep bank. Hawkeye drew a birch-bark canoe from its hiding place under some bushes and motioned to Alice and Cora and the singer.

When they were seated in the canoe, Hawkeye and Heyward paddled against the stream. The unhappy owner of the colt sat with a long face; the scout guided the canoe. Often he stopped to listen for any sounds that might come from the forest. Then, when satisfied that no enemy was near, he would slowly paddle on. Soon Heyward's eye caught sight of a number of dark objects under the high bank. He pointed them out to Hawkeye.

"I see them," said the scout. "Uncas and his father have hidden the horses here. Water leaves no trail, and even an owl couldn't find them in this dark hole."

Hawkeye pushed the canoe nearer the shore and spoke again with the Indians. The river at this point ran between high rocks, one of which stuck out directly over their heads. On the brow of the rocky cliff were tall trees, some of them with ragged limbs. Behind them could be seen only the dark curve of the bank, but in front the water seemed to pile up against the heavens and tumble into caves with a rush and roar that made the night a fearful one.

The horses had been tied to bushes that grew between the rocks. Here, standing in the water, they must spend the night. Now the scout stood up straight and steady in the rear of the canoe and, with his long pole, pushed against a rock and sent the light canoe into the middle of the tumbling stream. The struggle against the swift current was difficult, but those in the party had been told not even to lift a hand. They hardly dared breathe. Time after time they thought the spinning waters would sweep them to their death, but the strong hand of their

◇◇

guide kept the canoe moving ahead. Just as Alice closed her eyes in terror, thinking that they would be swept into the tumbling mass at the foot of the falls, the canoe floated to the side of a flat rock that lay on a level with the water.

"Where are we?" asked Heyward.

"At the foot of Glenn's Falls," [3] replied the scout. He could speak aloud now, for his voice would not carry beyond the roar of the water. "Now we must make a careful landing. If the canoe turns over, you will go down faster than you came up. Step out on the rock, all of you, and I'll go back for the Mohicans and the deer meat."

The canoe turned and disappeared in the heavy darkness. The travelers were afraid even to move along the broken rocks, for one false step might throw them into the roaring waters. But soon the canoe again rested close to the rock and Hawkeye and his Indian friends got out with their supplies.

"We are safe here," said Heyward cheerfully. "Did you see anything of the Hurons?"

"An Indian is a man to be felt before he is seen," re-

[3] *Glenn's Falls*, falls in the Hudson River, between Fort Edward and Fort William Henry.

turned Hawkeye as he climbed upon the rock carrying the deer that Uncas had shot. "When I am on the trail of Hurons, I trust other signs more than my eyes."

"Have they found our hiding place?" asked Heyward anxiously.

"I should be sorry to think so, but when we passed the horses they drew back as if they scented wolves—and a wolf is a beast that creeps close to an Indian hiding place."

"The wolves might smell this deer, or the dead colt might draw them," suggested Heyward.

"We had better cut up the meat and bring it into the cave and let the waste parts go down the stream. Otherwise we may have a pack of wolves howling for our deer, and Indians are quick to understand a wolf's howl."

Hawkeye, while talking, was preparing for something which his Indian friends seemed to understand. They moved silently with him to another part of the cave and disappeared against the dark face of the rock.

CHAPTER 6

Discovered by Indians

◇◇◇

HEYWARD and the girls watched anxiously while the scout and his Indian friends disappeared into the cave. Would these new guides be faithful or would they desert? But soon voices were heard. Then a flash of light showed the woodsmen far back among the rocks where Hawkeye was holding above his head a burning knot of pine. The light on his strong brown face and strange dress gave him an air both wild and charming. He was, indeed, a man of iron frame, quick eye, and keen mind.

The figure of Uncas, too, stood out clearly—straight, strong, and graceful—the perfect form often seen in the early Indians. His features were firm and high, his eye

◇◇◇

clear and fearless, his manner free and proud. Surely, they thought, such a young man would never allow himself to use his rich natural gifts to deceive or harm them.

"With such a noble youth for my guard," whispered Alice to Heyward, "I could sleep in peace."

"Let us hope that these Mohicans will not disappoint us," said Heyward, "and I do not believe they will."

Hawkeye motioned to the others to enter the cave. Then he spoke to Uncas. "This flame might light the Hurons to us. Drop the blanket over the opening." Then to the others he continued, "Here is a supper— not what Major Heyward and his friends have a right to expect, but I've seen the time when our soldiers were glad to eat deer meat raw. There's sassafras [1] branches for the ladies to sit on."

"Are we quite safe in this cave?" asked Heyward.

Just at that moment the Great Serpent stepped out of the darkness from behind Hawkeye. The shadows playing across his face gave him a look so ghostly that Alice cried out and even Cora rose to her feet. But the Indian only lifted another blanket, showing another opening. Then, with the fire held high above his head,

[1] *sassafras*, a bush or small tree, the branches of which bend easily and are pleasant to smell.

he crossed a deep narrow passage and entered another cave.

"Two caves, and two openings," said Hawkeye, laughing. "Old foxes like us aren't caught in a cave with only one door."

"Are we on an island here?" asked Heyward.

"Falls on both sides of us and the river above and below," answered Hawkeye.

While he was speaking, Uncas was waiting on the two girls, which was not the custom of Indian men. He brought Alice cool water in a gourd,[2] and deer meat in a trencher.[3] Hawkeye's eye never rested, but he ate with a hunger that nothing could disturb. Feeling sorry for the singer and his loss of the colt, he drew a small barrel from a cover of leaves and invited David to drink.

"Come, friend, and try a little of this. It will wash away thoughts of the colt and cheer you up. What do you call yourself?"

"Gamut—David Gamut," replied the singer, as he washed down his sorrows in a huge swallow of the powerful drink.

---

[2] *gourd*, a small fruit with a hard shell. With the seeds taken out, it can be used as a dish.

[3] *trencher*, a board hollowed out and used as a plate or serving dish.

"A very good name," said Hawkeye. "And what may be your calling?"

"I teach singing, especially the singing of psalms."

"Can you handle a gun?"

"Praise heaven!" exclaimed David, "I have never had to handle one. I follow none but my own high calling."

"A strange one," said Hawkeye, "but I suppose it's a gift. Can you sing us a friendly good night before the ladies go to sleep?"

"With great pleasure," said David. "What can be more fitting than to offer praise after being delivered from such dangers?"

He blew on his pitch pipe, and then he and the sisters sang a slow, sacred song which he had chosen as fitting for their thanks. The three voices, all true and rich and sweet, filled every corner of the cave with the beautiful air till the Indians thrilled to the music. They sat so still, with their eyes so set upon the rocks, that they seemed like men made of stone. Hawkeye, who seemed at first not to listen, was soon carried back to his childhood when he had heard such songs in the meeting house near his home. His firm face softened before the song was finished. Then as the last notes died away, another sound that seemed of neither heaven nor earth rose and cut through not only the cave but also the hearts of all who heard it.

"What was it?" asked Alice and Heyward together.

Hawkeye and the Indians listened closely. Then, when the sound was not repeated, they spoke together in low voices. Uncas slipped out of the cave and Hawkeye spoke:

"I did not think that there was any sound of man or beast that my ears had not heard, but this shows how wrong I was. It was not a war whoop. I know that well. But when such sounds are heard in the forest, one must take all care. The Mohicans and I will watch on the rocks. Let the ladies go to the inner cave and get some rest. We must leave here long before the sun is up, while the Mingoes are taking their morning nap."

"Is our danger so great?" asked Cora.

"If I knew what made that strange sound, I could tell you better. Even in battle we would know better what to do."

Uncas returned to say that he could see nothing. Nor did the light from the cave show outside. Their hiding place, he thought, had not been discovered. Still, Hawkeye was worried—and with reason, for soon the cry

❖◇

came again. Heyward, Hawkeye, and the Indians slipped out of the cave to listen, and again the awful sound arose as if from the bed of the river.

"Now that I hear it in the open I know what it is," said Heyward, "for I have often heard it on the field of battle. It is the horrid cry that a horse gives when it is in pain or in terror. My horse has been attacked by beasts or he sees them and cannot get away."

Hawkeye, after thinking a moment, said, "Wolves must be there on the bank. Uncas, drop down and throw live coals among them, or we'll lose the horses."

Uncas had started down to the water when a long howl was carried swiftly into the forest as if the wolves had already been frightened away. Uncas returned and the three seated themselves in the shadows to watch. The two sisters lay on the sassafras branches to get what sleep they could. Heyward placed himself at the opening of the cave where he could speak to the guards if necessary, and the singer crowded himself into an opening between two rocks, where he was soon making such sounds as would have shocked him in his waking moments.

Hours passed with Hawkeye and the two Indians lying as still as the rocks of which they seemed to form a part. Not a sound escaped them, but their eyes never closed. At last the moon set and a thin line of light showed that day was coming.

Then, for the first time, Hawkeye stirred. He wakened Heyward, who had fallen asleep, and whispered, "Now is the time to start. Wake the gentle ones. Be quiet, but be quick."

Even as Heyward wakened the girls, there arose yells that made his blood run cold. David stood up and with his hands over his ears, demanded, "What is this noise? Has all hell broke loose?"

There were quick reports from a dozen guns and the unhappy singer fell senseless on the rock where he had slept. The enemy sent up a wild cry of joy at this and the Mohicans boldly sent back their war cry. Hawkeye told all of his party to keep themselves under cover, and then he disappeared. Soon a stream of flame came from the rock below, and a fierce cry of pain told that Hawkeye's gun had hit its mark. The enemy quickly drew back into the woods and again all was still. Now Heyward ran to the body of David and carried him into the cave.

"The poor fellow is alive and he still has his scalp," said Hawkeye when he returned to the group, "but to

◇◇

show six feet of flesh and blood to those Mingoes was madness. Lay him there on the sassafras branches, and when he has slept awhile, he will come to himself and be a wiser man."

"Do you think they will come again?" asked Heyward.

"A hungry wolf won't be satisfied with one bite. They lost a man, and they will come again with new plans to get our scalps. Our main hope will be to hold this rock until Munro can send men to help us. God send them soon, and under a leader who knows Indian ways."

"We'll hope for the best," said Heyward. "Come inside, Cora. I'll see if I can help Hawkeye."

"Oh, Duncan!" exclaimed Cora, her lips trembling. "Remember your safety is necessary to ours. Father trusts you. So much depends upon you, and you are so dear to all of the name of Munro."

"If anything could add to my love for life," replied Heyward, "it would be to hear that. But, as an officer, I must take my part in this fight. It will not be hard, though. All we have to do is hold the enemy back a few hours." He slipped away then to join Hawkeye and the Indians. All four hid themselves among the rocks and the pines in the middle of the island.

As there were no signs of another attack, Heyward began to think the enemy had been driven off, but Hawkeye shook his head.

"The Hurons never quit without a scalp," he said. "From their yells this morning, I'd say there were forty of them. They know our numbers and they know we can't all fight." His eye searched the water. "Look! where the water breaks over the rocks. The devils have come to the end of this island. Keep close, or they'll kill us in no time!"

Four bloodthirsty redskins had reached the end of the island. A moment later another was seen swimming toward the same spot. He was already reaching out his arm to be helped by his companions when the swift current caught him and tossed him over the falls. Heyward's first thought was to rush out to save him, but the iron hand of Hawkeye held him back.

"Would you tell those Mingoes where we lie?" he demanded. "This saves us a charge of powder, which we need badly. Put fresh powder in your guns. The mist from the falls may wet the brimstone.[4] Then stand ready for a close battle while I fire on the first rush."

Uncas crept up to him. "I see them, boy, I see them!"

---

[4] *brimstone*, sulphur. It is used in making gunpowder and also in matches.

◇◇

exclaimed Hawkeye. "They are gathering for a rush. The first man will die, if it's Montcalm himself!"

At this moment four Hurons, screaming madly, leaped toward them. When they were only a few rods away, Hawkeye rose slowly from the brush and fired. The first Indian bounded and fell forward.

"Now, Uncas!" cried Hawkeye, "you take the last of the devils and we'll take the other two!"

He and Heyward fired together, but without success.

"I knew it!" said Hawkeye, throwing down his gun. "Come on, you dogs of hell!"

A fierce savage ran at him. They caught each other's wrists and each struggled with all his might. The hard muscles of the scout held like iron; slowly the Indian gave way. Then, with a mighty pull, Hawkeye freed his own right arm and drove a knife into the heart of his enemy.

In the meantime Heyward was caught in a more deadly struggle. Another savage had attacked him. During the first part of their fight, Heyward's sword had snapped and his safety depended entirely upon the strength of his body. Happily, he soon succeeded in disarming his foe, whose knife fell on the rocks at their feet. From this moment it became a fierce struggle who should throw the other over the rocks and into the falls. Nearer and nearer to the edge they came until each tottered on the very brink. Heyward felt the other's hand on his throat—he saw the savage smile of the Indian—he felt his own body give way to that great strength. But as death seemed near, a dark hand and a flashing knife appeared before him, blood flowed freely from the cut wrist of the red man, and Heyward was drawn back by the saving arm of Uncas. But there was no time to lose.

"Get under cover!" cried Hawkeye. "Our work is only half done!"

The young Mohican gave a loud cry of victory and, followed by Heyward, ran up the steep rocks and into the cave.

CHAPTER 7

The Powder Is Lost

◇◇◇

DURING the greater part of the battle between the four Hurons and Heyward's party, strong interest had kept the other Hurons quiet. But the moment they saw that their men were lost, they set up a fierce cry for revenge. Their rifles flashed as they fired at their foes. The Great Serpent remained at his post on the rock below and returned shot for shot. He answered Uncas' cry of victory with one shout, then settled down to firing at the best targets his eye could find. The Iroquois poured shot among them, but only David had been wounded.

"Let them burn their powder," said Hawkeye. "There will be plenty of lead to gather when it's all over. Uncas,

◇◇◇

you waste your powder by overcharging, and a kicking gun never carried a true bullet. I told you to hit that last fellow right below his line of white paint, and you missed it by two inches. The life lies low in a Mingo, but fair play tells us to make a quick end of them—even if they are serpents."

A quiet smile crossed the face of the young Mohican, showing that he understood what Hawkeye said, but he made no reply.

"Don't blame Uncas for being too hasty," said Heyward. "He saved my life in the coolest way, and I'll always owe him my thanks."

Partly raising himself on the rock, Uncas offered his hand to Heyward to show that he valued this friendship. Hawkeye said in a softer tone, "Friends in these woods owe each other their lives when they are in danger. I dare say I may have served Uncas some such turn myself, and I well remember that he has stood between me and death five times——"

A bullet whistled just over their heads. "That was well aimed," said Heyward, and Uncas pointed to the top of a tree that overhung the river just opposite them. In its very top was an Iroquois, only partly hidden by

◇◇

the topmost leaves and the old twisted trunk as he looked down on them.

"Those devils would fire from heaven if they could," said Hawkeye. "Keep them in play, boy, till I get my gun ready; then we'll try both sides of the tree at once."

The two guns flashed at the same time and leaves and bark flew, but the Indian answered with a wild laugh. At once wild screams burst from the woods and again bullets whistled over their heads.

"Uncas, call your father; we have need of all our weapons to bring that Huron down," said Hawkeye.

The Great Serpent came and spoke his usual "Hugh" when Uncas pointed out the man in the tree. They planned together for a moment, and then each took his place. The Huron kept up his fire from the tree and the bullets fell dangerously close. Heyward's clothes were cut, and once blood was drawn from a slight wound in his arm.

The Huron took a more deadly aim and both of the Mohicans fired back at once. After a moment of struggle, the savage was seen swinging in the wind, still hanging to a branch. The yells in the forest died out, for the eyes of all were fixed on the wounded Indian swinging

between heaven and earth. He sternly faced his foes with a look of cold hate. One hand lost its hold. Slowly the other hand slipped and the Huron fell into the water below. One yell burst from the woods; then all was still.

"And now the last charge in my horn is gone, and the last bullet is gone," said the unhappy Hawkeye. "Uncas, lad, go down to the canoe and bring up the big horn. It's all the powder we have left, and we'll need every grain of it."

A moment later the young Mohican gave a sharp cry and pointed down the river. Only a little way from the rock, their canoe was floating toward the middle of the

◇◇

stream, directed by someone in the water. Hawkeye
raised his rifle as if by habit, but it was of no use.

"It's too late, too late!" said Hawkeye bitterly, as he
dropped his gun beside him.

The tricky Huron raised his head above the side of
the canoe, waved his hand, and gave forth a yell that
was his signal of success. He was answered by a shout
and a laugh from the woods. The cunning plan had won.

"Laugh if you want to, you sons of hell!" cried Hawkeye. "The three quickest and truest guns in these woods
are no better now than last year's horns of a buck!" [1]

"What can we do now?" asked Heyward.

Hawkeye made no reply, but passed his finger around
the crown of his head, and everyone in the party understood what he meant.

"Surely we are not lost!" returned Heyward. "We
can keep those Hurons from landing."

"With what?" asked Hawkeye coolly. "With the arrows of Uncas? Or such tears as women shed? You are
young and rich and have friends; and at your age it is
hard to die. But let us teach those Iroquois that white
blood can flow as nobly as red."

---

[1] *last . . . buck.* The male deer (also the male of some other animals) loses its horns
each year and grows new horns the next year.

◇◇◇

From the manner of the Mohicans, Heyward knew what fate the party might expect. Great Serpent sat straight up on the rock, laid aside his knife and tomahawk, and moved to take the eagle's feather from his hair. He smoothed his scalp lock. His dark, flashing eyes were losing some of their fierceness.

"But not all hope is gone—it can't be!" cried Heyward. "Help may be near, and our enemies seem to have tired of the struggle in which they have gained so little!"

"It may be a minute or an hour before the snakes steal back," replied Hawkeye, "but they will come. There is little hope. Great Serpent, my brother, we have fought our last battle together. The Hurons will shout victory at the death of the wise man of the Mohicans, and also over their enemy, the paleface."

"Let their women weep over their dead!" returned the Indian proudly. "Eleven of their warriors lie hid from the graves of their tribe since the snows have melted, and none can tell where to find them when the tongue of Great Serpent is still. Let them draw their sharpest knives, for their most bitter enemy is now in their hands. Uncas, last of the noble Mohicans, call on the dogs to come soon, or their hearts will soften and they will change to women."

◇◇

"They look among the fishes for their dead," said the soft voice of the young chief. "They drop from the oaks like fruit that is ready to be eaten! And the Delawares laugh!"

"Aye, aye," said Hawkeye, "Great Serpent and Uncas have warmed their feelings and will soon call on the Iroquois to give them a quick end. As for me, I am of the blood of the whites. I want to die as a white man should, with no words of hate in my mouth and no bitterness in my heart!"

"Why die at all?" asked Cora, trying to hide her fear. "The path is open, and we owe too much to you already. Fly to the woods and save yourselves."

"Lady, you know little of the cunning of the Hurons if you think they have left any path open to the woods," replied Hawkeye. "And yet—the river would soon sweep us out of reach of their guns."

"Then try the river. Why stay here and be killed?"

"Why?" repeated the scout, looking at her proudly. "Because it is better for one to die at peace with himself than to live in fear. What could we say to Munro when he asks how we left his children?"

"Go to him and beg him to hurry back to our aid. Say that the Hurons have taken his daughters away but that speed may save them. If, after all, Heaven should not send aid in time, give him the love of his daughters. Tell him not to mourn for us, but to look forward with a Christian's faith that we shall meet again in heaven."

The hard, brown face of Hawkeye began to change as he listened.

"There is reason in her words!" he said. "And she shows a true Christian spirit. Great Serpent! Uncas! Did you hear what the dark-eyed woman has said?"

After the three had spoken together seriously for some minutes, the older Indian raised his hand and spoke the one word "Good!" Putting his knife and tomahawk in his belt, he walked to the edge of the rock and dropped into the water. Hawkeye stopped to speak to Cora.

"If you are spared and led into the woods," he said, "break the twigs on the bushes as you pass, and make your trail as plain as you can. I am your friend and will follow to the ends of the earth to save you." Then he added bitterly, "If our powder had held out, this shame would not have come upon us!" He dropped into the water and he, too, was gone.

◇◇

Cora turned to Uncas. "Your friends are gone and should be safe now. It is time for you to follow."

"Uncas will stay," said the young chief quietly.

"Your staying will make our chances of being saved much less. Go!" Cora's eyes fell under his steady look. "Go to my father as my secret messenger. Tell him to give you whatever is needed to buy the freedom of his daughters. It is my wish that you go!"

Unwilling though he was, Uncas turned away. "I go to your father," he said, and without a sound, he, too, was gone.

All this took only a few minutes. Cora turned next to Heyward.

"Duncan," she said with a trembling lip, "I have heard that you swim as well as they do. Follow their wise example."

"Is that the faith Cora Munro places in me?" he asked with a sad and bitter smile.

"Your duty demands that you go," she said. "You cannot help us here now, and your life may be saved for other friends."

He made no reply but looked down at Alice, who was clinging to his arm.

"Think," said Cora. "The worst that can happen to us is death and all of us must meet Death at some time."

"No," he answered, "there are things worse than death, and perhaps if I stay I can check them."

Without urging further, Cora placed an arm around her sister and drew her into the cave.

CHAPTER 8

Captured by the Hurons

◇◇◇

THE SUDDEN change from the exciting struggle to this complete quiet seemed to Heyward like a dream. Although with the going of Uncas every sign of hope seemed lost, yet Duncan began to feel more easy in his mind. From the rocks and forest came no sound of the enemy. The roar of battle that had filled the woods had died out, leaving only the rush of waters and the voices of nature. A fish hawk dived from the highest branches of a dead pine. A bluejay opened his throat to give forth his noisy calls.

"None of the enemy is in sight," said Heyward to David, who was still weak from his wound. "We'll hide in the cave and trust to God."

"I remember singing songs of praise and thanks with two lovely ladies," said the puzzled David. "But since then the anger of God has visited me, and in my sleep I heard shouts and unpleasant noises."

"Poor fellow! Come with me where you can hear nothing but your own singing."

Smiling sadly, David leaned on the arm of Heyward and entered the narrow mouth of the inner cave. Heyward hid the opening with sassafras branches, then hung blankets so that no light could pass through.

"I like the American saying, 'While life remains, there is hope,'" said Heyward, trying to quiet the fears of all the party. "Cora, you have both wisdom and courage. Now, if we can only give Alice more hope."

"I feel better, Duncan," said Alice through her tears. "In this cave we seem safe, and surely in good time our friends will bring us help."

"Now you talk like a daughter of Munro!" said Heyward, pressing her hand. Then, seating himself in the middle of the cave, he examined his one remaining gun, determined to make as good a stand as possible against any danger that might come. "If the Iroquois come back, they won't catch us as easily as they think," he muttered.

◇◇

As the minutes passed, all within the cave seemed in better spirits, but each knew the nature of the Indian and remembered stories of Indian cruelty—burning at the stake and other terrible killings. David, more cheerful than the others, opened his hymnbook and prepared to sing. "Isle of Wight," he said in the full, rich voice that had always held the respect of his pupils. "It is a brave tune and set to sacred words. Let us sing it now— sing it with respect."

"Isn't it dangerous to sing here?" asked Cora.

"His voice can't be heard above the sound of the falls," Heyward assured her.

David began the song and his voice, although still weak, seemed sweeter and more brave than ever. Alice dried her tears and Cora smiled at the singer. Heyward, instead of keeping his close watch on the opening of the cave, turned to look fondly at the still moist eyes of Alice. Then all at once there burst upon the air a wild yell that stopped the voice of the singer as if his heart had jumped into his throat.

"We are lost!" cried Alice, throwing her arms around her sister.

"Not yet," said Heyward. "That sound came from the center of the island, where they have found their dead companions. But they have not found us; there is still hope."

Quickly there came a second yell, then a rush of voices.

Cries and screams filled the island. Some called from the water's edge; answers came from the heights above. Cries came near the opening to the cave, and heavier yells arose out of the deep hollow.

In the midst of the uproar, a yell of success was raised very close to the cave. Heyward believed this to be a sign that they had been discovered, but other cries told that Hawkeye's rifle had been found. "The Long Rifle," shouted the Indians over and over again. Heyward knew that this name had been given by the Indians to a famous hunter and scout of the English camp, but only now did he learn that "The Long Rifle" was his late companion, Hawkeye.

The whole band of Hurons had gathered around this prize, which seemed to mean to them that their hated enemy had been killed. With loud bursts of savage joy they began a search for the body.

"Now," whispered Heyward to the trembling sisters, "now is the moment of doubt. If they do not find the opening, we are safe. We know that our friends have

◇◇◇

escaped, and within two hours they can bring help to us from Webb."

A few moments of awful stillness told Heyward that the Hurons were making a careful search. More than once he heard their footsteps as they brushed against the sassafras. At length the pile moved a little, a corner of the blanket dropped, and a ray of light fell into the cave. A shout told that the cave had been discovered. Then the voices of the whole band gathered around the secret place.

Pushing the others back into the shadows, Heyward placed himself in front of them to meet the first attack. David's wound had left blood on some of the sassafras leaves. Seeing this, the Indians set up a howl like dogs finding a trail. "The Long Rifle," they cried. They tore up the bed of the cave and carried branches out, scat-

tering them as if expecting to find there the body of the man they both hated and feared. For a time it seemed that the little band of whites would not be discovered. But suddenly Alice pointed in terror to a narrow shelf of rock above where she stood, and there was the fierce and savage face of Sly Fox.

The look of triumph that came over the face of the Fox so stirred Heyward's blood that he raised his gun and fired. The report of the gun in the hollow cave roared like thunder. When the smoke had cleared, Sly Fox was gone and a fearful silence followed. But soon there came a yell that nearly froze the blood of the little party of whites. Almost before they could catch their breath, they were dragged into the open and surrounded by the Hurons.

PART TWO

<><><><><><><><><><><><><><><><><><><><><><><><><><><><><><>

A wild flight
through
enemy lines

CHAPTER 9

Led into Captivity

◇◇

As HEYWARD began to recover from the shock of being dragged about, he began to study the savages who held his party prisoners. He was surprised to find that, unlike most Indians, these were showing some respect for him as well as for the trembling sisters. It was true—the younger ones had shown a great desire to take the rich ornaments from his uniform, but they were held in check by an older one who seemed to be in command. No immediate harm was attempted, and so Heyward felt sure that his party was being held for later punishment. The older warriors continued their search for victims and, not finding more, faced Heyward again, saying "The Long Rifle" with a fierceness that he well understood.

◇◇

The Fox alone showed no interest in the search but stood aside looking so satisfied that it was plain he felt he had already done what he most wanted to do. He now had these hated whites in his power. When the eyes of Heyward first met those of the Fox, he turned away in disgust, but checking that feeling, he spoke:

"Sly Fox is a good warrior. Surely he will tell a man who is not armed what these others are saying."

"They ask for the hunter who knows the paths through the woods," replied the Fox in broken English, at the same time laying his hand on the bundle of leaves that bound the wound on his shoulder. "The Long Rifle has good gun and his eye never shut. But, like short gun of white chief, it cannot take life of Sly Fox."

"Sly Fox is too brave to remember the hurts received in war, or the hands that gave them."

"Was it war when tired Indian rested at the sugar tree? Whose tongue talked peace while his heart was colored with blood? Did Sly Fox dig up hatchet?"

Sly Fox seemed quite pleased with himself, and Heyward did not think it wise to remind him that he had played false with those whom he had promised to guide through the woods. The other Indians again took up their cry of "The Long Rifle" when they saw this short talk had ended.

"You hear them call for the life of the Long Rifle?" asked the Fox. "If they do not get him, they will take the blood of the one that keeps him hid."

"He is gone."

"Is he bird to fly away? Is he fish to swim? White man read in books and think Indians fools!"

"The Long Rifle is not a fish, but he can swim. When the powder was all gone, he swam down the river."

"Why did white chief stay?" demanded the Fox. "Is he stone that cannot swim or is he tired of his scalp?"

Heyward tried now to wake in the Indian some respect for an enemy who had proved he could fight. "Your dead warrior who died at the falls could tell you that I am not a stone," he replied. "The white man does not desert his women."

"Where is Great Serpent?"

"He, too, has gone down the river."

"Where is Bounding Elk?"

"I do not know whom you mean," said Heyward.

"Uncas," returned the Fox. "Bounding Elk is what white man call him."

◇◇

"If you mean the young Delaware, he, too, has gone down with the water."

The Fox seemed satisfied with these answers, and the other Indians gathered around to learn what he had heard. The Fox pointed to the river, explaining the escape. The Hurons, seeing that they had lost their game, were thirsty for revenge. Some of them ran madly to the water, making wild motions. Some looked angrily at the prisoners. One of them took hold of Alice's hair, which hung in rich folds over her shoulders, and waved his knife around her head as if to take her scalp. Heyward sprang to her side, but the powerful Indian in command of the band caught his shoulder in a strong grip.

Heyward knew it would be impossible for him to escape the Iroquois, and so he tried to cheer the sisters. Now he was relieved to see the leader call his men for a council. They seemed to think that help might come from Webb's camp, for several times during their meeting they pointed toward Fort Edward. Soon they agreed upon a plan. A canoe was brought near the mouth of the cave and the leader made signs to the prisoners to get into it.

Heyward went first and was followed by the sisters and the still puzzled David. The Indians then paddled a short way down the stream and landed the prisoners on the south bank of the river, nearly opposite where they had struck it the night before.

Here the Indians again held a council. The horses, whose fear had brought the Indians, were led from the cover of the woods and the band now divided. The great chief mounted Heyward's horse and led the way directly across the river. His party followed him into the woods, leaving the prisoners in charge of six savages, one of whom was Sly Fox. Heyward began to grow more uneasy. What were the Indians planning?

Wanting to know the worst, he wondered if gold and flattery would make the Fox talk.

"I would speak to Sly Fox what is fit for only a great chief to hear."

Looking back with scorn, the Indian said, "Speak. Trees have no ears."

"Sly Fox has proved himself worthy of the name given to him by his Canadian fathers," began Heyward. "I see his wisdom in all that he has done for us. I shall remember when the hour comes to reward him. Yes,

◇◇◇

Sly Fox has proved himself not only a great chief, but
one who knows how to deceive his enemies."

"What has Sly Fox done?" asked the Indian coldly.

"Did he not see that the woods were filled with the
enemy so that not even a serpent could steal through
without being seen? Did not Sly Fox pretend to lose his
way so he might blind the eyes of the Hurons? Did he
not pretend to go back to his tribe, who had treated
him badly and driven him from their wigwams like a
dog? And did not we, when we saw what he wished to
do, help him when we shot at him? We made the Hurons
think he was our enemy. Does not Sly Fox mean to turn
like a fox and carry these two daughters to the rich
Scotchman?"

"You think Sly Fox did all this?"

"Yes," replied Heyward, "I see it all, and I am thinking how to pay for such wisdom and honesty. The Fox
shall have money of solid gold. He shall have plenty of
powder in his horn. I do not know how to show more
thanks than the Scotchman, but I—yes, I will——"

"What will the young chief give?" demanded Sly Fox.

"He will make firewater flow before wigwam of Sly
Fox, until the heart shall be lighter than the down of

feathers and his breath shall be sweeter than the wild flowers."

The Fox listened gravely and thought deeply. Then, laying his hand on his wounded shoulder, he said, "Do friends make such marks?"

"Does the Long Rifle ever miss his aim when he really wants to kill?" returned Heyward, smiling.

"Enough. Go, but keep mouth shut. When Sly Fox speaks, then will be time to answer."

The Fox went to the horses and motioned to Heyward to help the sisters into their saddles. Not knowing how to delay any longer, Heyward expressed hope to Alice and Cora, who, in their fear, could hardly raise their eyes from the ground. As David's horse had been taken away by the great chief, David, like Heyward, had to walk. But Heyward decided that walking was better than riding, for they would journey more slowly and have a better chance of getting help from Webb. When all was ready, the Fox gave the order to start. He led the

way. David followed, then the sisters and Heyward, with the Indians at each side and behind them watching lest the prisoners might try to escape. And so they went on toward the south.

Although their course lay nearly opposite to the road to Fort William Henry, Heyward could hardly believe that his offer had so soon been forgotten. Knowing what a winding path an Indian can take when he wants to be careful, he believed that they would at last turn and reach Webb's camp. However, mile after mile passed in suffering without any seeming end to the journey. Sometimes Heyward fancied the Fox was afraid to pass Montcalm's army and meant, instead, to deliver his prisoners to a certain English officer who was a friend of the evil Hurons. Even this would be better than being led into Canada, but, had Heyward only known it, every step was carrying him farther from his post of honor and duty.

Cora alone remembered the last words of the scout.

◇◇

Whenever it was possible, she bent aside such twigs as she could reach, but the close watching of the Indians made this difficult and dangerous. Once she broke a small branch of sumac and, at the same time, let her glove fall. One of the Indians picked up her glove and broke the branch completely off. Then, angrily laying his hand on his tomahawk, he made her understand that such signs must end. There was no hope now of leaving marks that would guide help toward them.

Guided by the sun and such small marks as the Indians knew, they crossed stretches of pine, little valleys, brooks, and wooded hills. The Fox never seemed to doubt his way. He never seemed to tire. He was always in the lead, the feather on his headdress flying in the wind.

But the Fox had an object in view. After crossing a brook, they climbed a hill so steep that the sisters had to get off their horses in order to follow. When they reached the top, they found themselves on a level spot thinly covered with trees. Under one of these trees, Sly Fox was already lying down as if ready and willing to take the rest so much needed by the whole party.

CHAPTER 10

Sly Fox Plans His Revenge

◇◇

ALTHOUGH the party had moved swiftly, one of the Indians had shot a deer and had carried, on his shoulders, the better part of the animal. Without waiting to cook the meat, he and his fellows were stuffing themselves with it, but Sly Fox did not join them. He was sitting alone in deep thought, and so Heyward moved over to talk to him.

"The Fox has gone far enough to escape Montcalm, has he not? And will not the chief of William Henry be better pleased to see his daughters soon? Then will the reward be greater."

"Gray-head chief is hard on warriors. Is his heart soft?"

"You have seen him in front of his soldiers, and I have seen his eyes wet with tears when he spoke of those daughters who are now in your power."

Over the Indian's face came a look that Heyward did not understand—he thought at first it was caused by a desire for gold. Then he feared that some deeper purpose was taking shape.

"Go to the dark-haired daughter," said the Fox coldly. "Say that Sly Fox waits to speak."

Heyward now wondered if the Indian wished to ask for more gifts. And so he spoke to Cora.

"You know what the Indians like," he said. "Offer him plenty of powder and blankets. On your offer and his feeling toward you may depend not only your life, but that of Alice as well."

"Yes, Duncan, and yours, too."

"My life is already sold to my king," returned Heyward. "Hush!" Then he spoke again to the Fox: "The lady is here."

The Indian rose slowly and looked at her a moment. Then, motioning Heyward away, he said coldly, "When Indian talks to woman, his tribe shut ears."

After Heyward had gone, Cora turned to the Indian

◇◇

and said, "What would Sly Fox say to the daughter of Munro?"

"Listen," said the Indian. He laid his hand firmly on her arm, but Cora quickly drew it away. "The Sly Fox was born chief of red Hurons on the lakes. He saw twenty snows of winter run off in streams before he ever saw paleface. And he was happy. Then white fathers came and taught the Sly Fox to drink firewater, and he grew cunning. The Hurons, his own people, drove him from the land of his fathers as they hunt buffalo. He ran down shores of lake and followed river to City of Guns.[1] He hunt and fish there till people chase him again through woods into arms of enemies. The chief, who was born Huron, became warrior among Mohawks."

"I have heard about that," said Cora, noting the rising anger of the Fox.

"Who gave Sly Fox firewater? Who made him bad Indian? It was white man—people of your color."

"But I cannot be blamed if bad people of my color have done this," said Cora.

"No—Sly Fox is a man, not a fool. The Great Spirit has made you wise."

[1] *"City of Guns,"* Indian name for Quebec.

"But what can I do to help you—to correct these wrongs?" asked the girl.

"Listen," said the Indian. "When English and French fathers dug up hatchet, Sly Fox went against his own nation. The white men drive Indians from hunting grounds, and now when they fight, a white man leads the way. The old chief, your father, was great captain in our war party. He said to Mohawks 'Do this' and they do it. He made law that if Indian drink firewater, it bad for him. Sly Fox foolish then. He drink it. He was led to cabin of Munro. What did the gray-head do? Let his daughter say."

"He did justice," said Cora. "He punished the one who used the firewater."

"Justice!" exclaimed the Indian. "Is it right to make firewater and then punish for it? The Fox was not himself—firewater acted for him. He was tied up before palefaces and whipped like dog."

Cora said nothing, not knowing how to answer this.

"See!" continued the Indian, tearing away the cloth that covered his chest. "Here are marks of knives and bullets. Indian proud of these, but your father left marks on back of chief that he must hide, like squaw."

◇◇

"An Indian's spirit should not feel the pain his body suffers," said Cora.

"When Chippewas [2] tied the Fox to tree and cut this wound," said the Fox, laying his finger on a deep mark, "Fox laughed in their faces and called them women. Then his spirit was in clouds! But when he felt blows of Munro, his spirit lay on ground under tree. The spirit of Huron never forgets."

"But if my father did not do you justice, show him how an Indian can forgive. Take his daughters back to him."

The Fox shook his head.

"What would you have?" asked Cora.

"What a Huron loves—good for good; bad for bad."

"Then you would revenge that wrong by hurting his daughters, who cannot help themselves? Would it not be more like a man to go before Munro's face and demand justice like a man?"

"Guns of palefaces are long! Why should the Fox go among them when he hold spirit of gray-head in his hand?"

---

[2] *Chippewas,* another Indian tribe, some living in Canada and some in what is now the United States.

"Will nothing soften your heart? At least let my sister go and punish me only."

"The light eyes can go back to her father and tell him what has been done, if the dark-haired woman will swear by the Great Spirit of her fathers to tell no lie."

"What must I promise?" asked Cora with a quiet dignity that puzzled the Fox.

"When Sly Fox left his people, his wife was given to another chief. Must he go back alone to his tribe? Let daughter of Munro follow and live in wigwam forever."

In spite of her horror, Cora forced herself to ask quietly, "What pleasure would Sly Fox find in having a wife he did not love—one of a different color and nation? It would be better to take gold of Munro and buy heart of Huron maid."

The Indian's reply was a look of perfect hate. "When blows cut the back of Huron, he knew then where to find woman to feel the hurt. The daughter of Munro would draw his water, plant his corn, and cook his meat. The body of the gray-head would sleep among his guns, but his heart would lie near the knife of Sly Fox."

"Beast!" she cried, in a burst of anger. "Only a devil could think of such revenge. Munro will crush you!"

◇◇

The Indian, smiling scornfully, motioned her away and returned to his friends. Heyward ran to Cora to ask the result of her talk with the Fox. But she could only point to the band of Indians and say, in a voice which she could not control, "There, there, read our fate in their faces! We shall see; we shall see!"

The Fox spoke to the savages, who were still stuffing themselves with the raw deer meat. They listened closely. His voice, at first low, rose higher and higher as he told of the wrongs the Indians had suffered. He spoke of their warriors, their merits, their battles, their wounds. He spoke of the Long Rifle, and shouts from the others filled the woods. Pointing to the prisoners, he told of the brave who had been shot from the branches of the tree. He told of the deaths of the others. Then, lifting his voice to a high, forced pitch, he cried:

"Are the Hurons dogs? What shall we say to those whose warriors were killed? What shall we say to the old men when they ask for scalps? The women will point their fingers at us. The dark spot on the names of the Hurons must be hid in blood!"

With revenge in their grasp, the whole band now sprang to their feet shouting, and rushed upon the

prisoners with knives drawn and tomahawks raised.
Heyward placed himself between the sisters and the
leader. Two powerful warriors threw themselves on him,
while another took hold of David. Neither was taken
without a struggle—even David threw his man to the
earth. After a hard fight, Heyward was bound to a
young tree and at the right Cora was bound to another.
She was pale and frightened, but she looked steadily at
her enemies. Alice, too, was tied to a tree and, but
for the cords that held her, would have fallen to the
ground. Her hands were joined in prayer, but her eyes
were turned to Heyward as if he alone could save them.

Now the plans of revenge were changed. Some of the
Hurons carried in branches to build up the fire. One cut
sharp sticks to pierce the flesh of the victims. Others
bent the tops of two small trees to bind Heyward to the
branches. Sly Fox spoke again to Cora, pointing out the
fate that would be hers.

"Ha!" he said. "What says the daughter of Munro?
Her head is too good to find a pillow in the wigwam of
Sly Fox. Will she like it better if it is fed to the wolves?"

"What does this beast mean?" cried the angry Heyward.

◇◇◇

"Nothing," said Cora. "He is a savage and knows not what he says. Let us, with our dying breath, pray for pardon for him."

"Pardon!" cried the Indian, thinking Cora meant to ask it of him. "The Indian's mercy is shorter than the white man's justice! Shall I send the yellow-hair back to her father, and will you go to the great lakes with Sly Fox to carry his water and feed him with corn?"

"Leave me," said Cora, again with that dignity which stopped the Fox for a moment. "You put bitterness into my prayers."

But soon the Fox spoke again, pointing to Alice: "The child weeps. She is young to die. Send her to Munro to keep life in the heart of the old man."

"Did he speak of sending me to Father, Cora?"

"Alice, he offers life to both of us, and to Duncan. You can go free if—if I will go——" Her voice broke.

"Dearest Cora," said Alice, "I wish the offer had been made to me. To save you and Duncan and to cheer Father, how willingly could I die."

"Die!" cried Cora. "To die would be easy. But he would have me follow him to the woods and remain with the Hurons. He would have me for his wife. Is life worth such a price? Alice and Duncan, tell me what to do, for I am all yours."

"Cora!" cried the young man in surprise and horror. "The very thought is worse than a thousand deaths!"

"I knew that you would answer so," said Cora with her eyes bright and her color mounting. "What says my Alice?"

Alice's head moved slowly. "No, no, no, better that we die as we have lived—together!"

"Then die!" shouted the Fox, throwing his tomahawk at Alice and grinding his teeth with rage. The ax passed in front of Heyward's face, cut some of the curls from Alice's hair, and buried itself in the tree above her head. Maddened to his greatest efforts, Heyward snapped the cords that held him and rushed upon another Indian who was aiming a blow. The Indian fell, but Heyward could not hold on to the naked body. The savage rose with one knee on Heyward's chest, pressing him down with the weight of a giant. Heyward had already seen a knife flashing in the air when he heard the whistle of a bullet and the crack of a rifle, and the Indian fell dead at his side.

CHAPTER 11

A Dangerous Foe Escapes

◇◇◇

TERROR seized the Hurons as they heard the report and saw one of their number so quickly killed. They knew that the bullet that went so straight to its mark could come from only one enemy, and at once there went up the cry, "The Long Rifle!" This cry was answered by a shout from the bushes where the Indians had piled their arms. At the next moment, Hawkeye was seen running in upon them. Too eager to stop and load the gun he had caught up from the pile, he rushed in swinging it around his head like a club.

Although he moved swiftly, another form bounded past him and leaped into the very center of the Hurons. There the figure stood whirling a tomahawk in one hand

❖❖

and a knife in the other. The Hurons fell back with cries of "Bounding Elk!" "Great Serpent!"

Uncas answered the cry. Leaping on one of his enemies, with one blow of his tomahawk he split his head open to the brain. Heyward, now free, seized the tomahawk that the Fox had just buried in the young tree. Each man singled out an enemy. Blows passed like the rush of the wind. Hawkeye soon got another Huron within reach of his arm and, with one sweep of his gun, crushed him to the ground. Heyward, overanxious, threw his tomahawk too soon. It struck the forehead of the Indian coming at him, but checked him for only a moment. Then Heyward sprang upon his foe with naked hands, but found that it took all of his strength and courage to fight off the terrible thrusts made by the knife of the Huron. As he was fast tiring, he heard a welcome voice near: "Kill the varlets! [1] Kill the Mingoes!"

The next moment Hawkeye's gun fell like a club on the Indian's head, and he sank to the earth, dead.

Uncas, having brained his first Huron, turned like a hungry lion to seek another. The fifth Huron, the only one not already matched in fight, sprang toward the helpless Cora, throwing his sharp ax on ahead of him.

[1] *varlet*, a low, mean person.

It touched her shoulder and cut the cords that bound her. Now free, she ran to Alice, but the savage followed, seized her by the hair, and threw her roughly to her knees. Drawing her flowing curls through his hand and raising them on high, he waved one arm, passing his knife around the head of his prisoner.

He laughed coarsely, but his joy was short, for Uncas had seen him threaten Cora. Bounding into the air, Uncas appeared to fall upon the Huron from the clouds, knocking him to the ground. Uncas closed with him, but the tomahawk of Heyward and the gun of Hawkeye came down on the head of the Indian. The next moment, the knife of Uncas had reached the red man's heart.

During all this time Sly Fox and Great Serpent had been engaged in a hand-to-hand fight, each one proving that well did he deserve the name given him. They had run at each other, closed, and twisted about each other like two serpents. The air was full of dust and leaves as if from a strong wind.

Heyward and his companions rushed about them. Uncas tried to drive his knife into the heart of the Fox.

Hawkeye raised his gun to strike. Heyward tried to seize the legs of the Huron. But the two were so covered with dust and blood, they moved so swiftly, that it was impossible to strike at the enemy without grave danger of hitting the friend. The Fox knew that he was more than matched. To escape the one would mean to fight the others. To save himself he would have to use cunning. Slowly he moved the fight from the center to the edge of the little plain. When Great Serpent saw a chance to make a thrust with his knife, the Fox loosened his hold and fell back as if dead. With a shout, the Serpent leaped to his feet.

"Well done for the Delawares!" cried Hawkeye. "I'll finish him with a blow from my gun. That won't rob the Mohican of his right to the scalp!"

But in that brief moment when Hawkeye was raising his rifle, the Fox rolled swiftly over the cliff. Springing to his feet, he was seen to leap into the bushes far below. The Delawares cried out in surprise and followed, but a sharp call from Hawkeye brought them back.

"It was like the Fox—lying varlet that he is," said Hawkeye. "Let him go. He's only one man without a gun and many miles from his French aids. Like a snake without its poison, he can do no more harm, and we have a long way to go. See, Uncas, your father is already taking the scalps. You might feel those 'dead' Mingoes or we may lose another."

Hawkeye freed David, and then he made the circle of the dead, thrusting his knife into the bodies as coolly as if they had been dead animals. But Uncas, unlike most Indians, had run with Heyward to Alice. They cut the cords that bound her and placed her in the arms of Cora. The girls fell upon their knees and words could not tell how gladly and how deeply they returned thanks to their Maker for being now returned to life and to each other.

Great Serpent began a search among the guns left by the Hurons and found his own as well as that of his son. All armed themselves with freshly loaded guns, and the party prepared to move. The sisters had quieted themselves and, with the help of Heyward and Uncas, now made their way down the hill that had so nearly been the scene of their death. The horses were found feeding at the foot of the hill, and, having mounted, the party followed Hawkeye. Soon he left the blind path that the Indians had used, turned into a thicket, crossed a brook, and stopped under the shade of a few elms.

The scout and the Indians seemed to know the spot

well. Leaning their guns against the trees, they began throwing aside the dry leaves with their hands and digging into the blue clay. Soon a spring bubbled up. The white man looked about as if expecting to find something which was not there.

"Them careless Hurons!" he muttered. "They have thrown away the gourd! Here the Lord has raised a spring of water better than medicine, but those robbers have stamped around here and have left the place unclean, as if they were beasts instead of men."

But Uncas found the gourd, took a long drink, handed the gourd to Hawkeye, and then began to examine the food which the Hurons had left.

"Look at this," said Hawkeye. "Those varlets know the better parts of the deer—and they might have cooked some of it, but everything is raw, for the Hurons are real savages. Uncas, take my steel and start a fire.[2] A bite of meat will taste good after so long on the trail."

"How did you find us so soon, and without help from the fort?" asked Heyward.

"If we had gone to the fort, we might have been too late to save your scalps," replied Hawkeye coolly. "No,

---

[2] *take . . . fire.* Steel struck against a hard stone throws out a spark. This spark can be caught on dry wood and fanned into a flame.

instead of throwing away strength by crossing to the fort, we lay under the bank of the Hudson to watch the direction of the Hurons."

"Then you saw all that happened?"

"Not all. Indian sight is too sharp, but we kept close. It was hard to keep Uncas in hiding. Uncas, you acted more like a curious woman than a warrior smelling his game."

"You saw us taken by the Indians?" asked Heyward.

"We heard you," said Hawkeye. "An Indian yell is plain language to a man of the woods. But when you got out of the canoe you were close to us and we had to creep like foxes or the Indians would have seen us. And then we lost sight of you till we saw you tied to the trees."

"How fortunate for us that you did not take the wrong path!" said Heyward. "The Hurons divided and there were horses on both paths."

"And we might have lost the trail because of that, if it had not been for Uncas. He had noticed that the horses ridden by the ladies planted both legs of one side on the ground at the same time. No other animal I know does that except the bear."

"These horses come from the shores of Narragansett

◇◇◇

Bay, and have that peculiar movement," said Heyward, who knew horses well. "But other horses are sometimes trained to travel that same way."

"Maybe," said Hawkeye, who seemed much interested in this explanation. "Though I am a white man, I know the forest animals better than horses. Well, next our trail hit a broken bush. One branch was bent up, as a lady breaks a flower from a stem. The rest were broken down as if the strong hand of a man had torn it. So I decided the Hurons had seen the twig bent and had torn the rest to make us think a deer had broken it."

"A smart way of figuring it out," said Heyward, "and you were right."

"And then it struck me that the Hurons would push for this spring, for they know how good the water is. Taste it for yourself."

Heyward took a little of the water and found it very bitter. Hawkeye laughed.

"You learn to like it. I've come to want it as much as the deer wants the licks.[3] It's better than wine to the red man, especially when he is sick. But Uncas has his fire burning and we must eat, for our journey is long."

[3] *licks*, places where salt is found on the earth, and where animals come to lick it up.

After their simple meal, each one took a long drink from the spring. Then the sisters mounted, Heyward and David took their guns, Hawkeye led, and the Mohicans brought up the rear. The party moved swiftly over the path toward the north.

CHAPTER 12

Night in the Old Blockhouse[1]

◇◇

HAWKEYE led his party in the direction opposite to that taken by the Fox. The way led, therefore, across the same plains and valleys and hills they had traveled that morning. The sun had now fallen low toward the distant mountains, but long before it grew dark the party had covered many miles on their return.

Hawkeye traveled rapidly, never seeming in doubt as to the way. The moss on the trees, the setting sun, the direction of the streams—all these helped him find his path. Now the forest began to change its colors— bright greens gave way to the darker greens of evening;

[1] *blockhouse*, a log house with holes between the logs. Through these holes, guns could be fired at an enemy.

a flood of golden glory touched the sinking sun; the clouds above the western hills were slowly edged with shining yellow.

"There in the sky is the sun telling us to seek food and rest," said Hawkeye. "But our night will soon be over, for with the moon we must be up and moving. I remember fighting the Mohawks here in the first war in which I ever drew blood. We threw up logs for a block-house to keep the varlets from getting our scalps. The place must be near here."

The hunter moved into a heavy thicket, pushing aside the branches that nearly covered the ground. His memory served him well, for within a few hundred feet he came upon an open space that surrounded a low green hill, on the top of which was, indeed, the old block-house. The roof had long since fallen, but the walls were still standing. Hawkeye and the Indians entered eagerly, Great Serpent proudly telling his son of the battle there and the part he himself had played in winning it. The sisters prepared to enjoy the safety of the cool spot, but Heyward asked:

"Could we not rest more safely in a place not so well known?"

◇◇

"Few live who know that this blockhouse was ever raised," said Hawkeye. "Not often do we hear of such battles as were fought here between the Mohawks and the Mohicans. I was just a boy, and went out with the Mohicans because I knew they had been wronged. Forty days and forty nights we were behind this pile of logs. We killed two for one till our numbers were about equal. Then we struck out at the dogs, and not a man of them ever got back to tell what became of the party. Yes, I was young then and new to the sight of blood. I didn't want spirits like my own to lie on the naked ground and have their bones whiten in the sun, so I buried the dead myself, on this little hill where we now sit—a seat raised by the bones of men."

Heyward and the two sisters arose quickly, a little cry of horror escaping the girls. Hawkeye, smiling at their alarm, continued:

"They are gone. They will never shout again or strike another blow. Great Serpent and I are the only living men who know they are here. The brothers and family of the Mohican formed our war party, and before you now you see all that are left of the Mohican race."

The eyes of the listeners turned to the two Indians with a deep sympathy and interest in their lonely fortunes, while the father went on calmly but proudly telling his story to Uncas.

They found a spring which, years before, had led the Mohicans to choose this spot for their blockhouse. They cleared away the leaves and cool, pure water bubbled up. Alice and Cora drank from this and ate some of the meat which their guides had prepared. Then they lay down within the walls of the old building and were soon asleep. Heyward made ready to pass the night on guard outside, but Hawkeye pointed to Great Serpent.

"The eyes of a white are too heavy and too blind for such a watch. The Mohican will keep watch for us tonight. Sleep, like Uncas and me. You will be safe."

Knowing that he could not change the mind of the scout, Heyward sat with his back against the logs of the blockhouse. But he was determined not to close an eye until he had seen the girls safe with their father. Hawkeye soon fell asleep and all was quiet.

Heyward tried to keep his senses alive to every sound of the forest. He saw the stars glittering overhead, the sleeping forms of his companions, Great Serpent sitting up straight and still as one of the trees. He heard a night bird's song along with the call of an owl, but slowly sleep overcame him. How long he slept, he did not know, but he was wakened by a light tap on his shoulder.

"Who comes?" he demanded. "Friend or enemy?"

"Friend," said the voice of Great Serpent. "Moon comes, and white man's fort is far, far off. When sleep shuts eyes of Frenchmen, time to move."

"I'm ready," said Heyward. "Call your friends and saddle the horses while I wake the sisters."

"We are awake, Duncan," Alice spoke softly from within the building. "We have had a good sleep, but you have watched through the night—and after a hard day."

"You mean I should have watched. After leading you into this danger by my poor judgment, I can't even keep awake to guard you."

"Only you would blame yourself for that," said Alice, but they were interrupted by Hawkeye.

"The Mohicans hear an enemy!" he whispered, seizing his gun.

"Probably some animal of the forest looking for food," said Heyward in a low voice.

"Listen!" returned Hawkeye. "It's man—I can tell

his footsteps. That thieving Huron has fallen in with one of Montcalm's parties, and they have found our trail. I don't like to draw any more blood, but what must be, must be! Lead the horses into the blockhouse, Uncas. And, friends, go to the same shelter. It's poor and old, but it offers a cover."

The sound of footsteps could now be heard clearly. They were soon mixed with voices calling to each other in an Indian tongue.

"Hurons!" whispered Hawkeye.

When the Indians reached the point where the horses had entered the thicket around the blockhouse, they paused, seeming to have lost the marks that guided them. By their voices there might have been twenty of them—all talking at once.

"The devils know our weakness," whispered Hawkeye, peering through an opening in the logs, "or they wouldn't have come on such a squaw's march. Listen to the low-down snakes!"

Heyward held his gun more firmly and fastened his eyes anxiously on the narrow opening. The deep voice of one who seemed to be the leader was heard. Then the scattered snapping of twigs showed that the Indians had separated to look for the trail. They did not find it, and before long they were beating about in the bush, coming nearer and nearer to the little circle of trees that hid the anxious group.

"They are coming," whispered Heyward. "Let us fire as soon as they are near enough."

"Keep everything hidden," returned Hawkeye. "The snapping of a flint or the smell of a single grain of powder would bring the hungry varlets upon us in a body. If we must give battle to save our scalps, trust to men who know the ways of these savages and are not afraid when the war whoop is howled."

Heyward looked behind him and saw the two sisters trembling in the corner, while the two Mohicans stood in the shadow straight and still—ready to strike whenever a blow might be needed. While he peered out, the bushes opened and a tall, armed Huron walked into the open space. As he looked upon the silent blockhouse, the moon fell upon his bronzed face and showed his complete surprise. With a grunt, he called his companion to his side.

For several moments these two stood together talking in their own tongue. Then they stepped forward carefully—like frightened deer—till they reached the rounded grave where so many of their people were buried. Hawkeye loosened his knife and lowered his gun; Heyward prepared himself for the struggle he thought was sure to come.

The savages were so near that any motion of the horses or a breath louder than common would have given them away. But the Hurons seemed to understand what the mound was. They spoke in low, solemn voices—they drew back, keeping their eyes on the ruins as if they expected to see the dead rise from those silent walls. Then they slowly moved back into the brush and disappeared. Hawkeye dropped his gun and drew a long, free breath.

"Aye! They respect their dead," he said. "This time it has saved their lives, and maybe the lives of better men."

Great Serpent listened closely while Hawkeye waited. Then at a sign from the scout, he motioned to Heyward to lead the horses out. They helped the sisters to mount and, stealing out toward the north, they left the falling ruins and buried themselves in the darkness of the heavy forest.

CHAPTER 13

Safe under the Guns of the Fort

◇◇

THE PATH became more rough as the mountains closed in on both sides of them. Suddenly Hawkeye made a stop and, in the quiet darkness, spoke in a low voice:

"It is easy to know the paths and to find the licks and water courses. But who would think that a mighty army is resting among those silent trees and bare mountains?"

"Then we are near William Henry?" asked Heyward.

"A long, hard path yet, and when and where to strike is now our greatest problem. See," pointing through the trees to a spot where a body of water lay shining under the stars, "there is the 'bloody pond.' I've traveled often around here, and I've fought the enemy from rising to setting sun."

"You have seen much service on this front?" asked Heyward.

"Aye!" said the scout proudly. "There are few hills here that haven't rung with the crack of my rifle, and there is little space between the Horicon [1] and the river where my Killdeer [2] hasn't dropped a living body, be it enemy or beast. But listen! Do you see something walking on the shore of the pond?"

"We are not likely to see anyone in this lonely forest," said Heyward.

"By heaven! there is a human form and it is coming toward us!" said Hawkeye. He gripped Heyward's shoulder with a strength that told the young soldier that terror of spirits had seized the older man. "Stand to your arms, my friends."

"Qui vive?" [3] came a sharp voice out of the dark.

"France!" replied Heyward, who, fortunately, could speak French.

"Where do you come from, and where are you going at this early hour?" demanded the voice, still in French.

"I come from a hiding place, and I must soon go to bed," said Heyward.

---

[1] *Horicon*, now Lake George.
[2] *Killdeer*, Hawkeye's rifle.
[3] *Qui vive* (kē vēv), French for "Who goes there?"

◇◇

"Are you an officer of the King?"

"Without a doubt, my friend," answered Heyward. "I am a captain. I have here the two daughters of Colonel Munro. I made them prisoners near the other fort, and I am taking them to our general. You have heard of them?"

"Upon my faith, ladies, I am sorry for you," exclaimed the young soldier, touching his cap. "Such is the fortune of war! But you will find our general a very fine man, and very polite to the ladies."

"That is always true of a good soldier," said Cora. "Good-by, my friend, I could wish you more pleasant duty."

The soldier made a bow as they left. The party moved forward, leaving the guard pacing the banks of the pond, singing to himself a song which was brought to his mind by the sight of the ladies and by thoughts of his own beautiful France.

"It's a good thing you speak French," said Hawkeye. "And it's a good thing he was friendly or a place might have been found for his bones among the other French dead."

There was a heavy groan from the bank of the pond.

"That sounded human," said Hawkeye.

"It *was* human," said Heyward, looking around and missing Great Serpent from their little band.

Another groan more faint was followed by a heavy plunge into the water, and all was still again. While they still wondered, the form of the Indian came stealing out of the brush. With one hand he tied the scalp of the unhappy French soldier to his belt; with the other he put back his knife and tomahawk. Then he took his place in the rear with the air of a man who had done a good deed.

Hawkeye stood in deep silence for a moment. Then, shaking his head, he said as if to himself: "That would have been a cruel act in a white man but the Indian does not understand. I could wish it had been a cursed Mingo instead of a young French soldier."

"It is done," said Heyward, wishing that it had not happened and also wishing to go on before the sisters should learn about it. "Better not done, but we cannot help him now. What are your plans?"

"Yes," said Hawkeye, pulling himself together. "As you say, it is too late to help him now. The French have gathered around the fort, and we have a small needle to thread [4] in passing them."

---

[4] *small needle to thread*, difficult work that must be done very carefully.

◇◇

"And but little time," added Heyward, with a quick look at the moon.

"We could turn the horses loose," said Hawkeye. "Then, by sending the Mohicans on in front, we might cut a lane through the guards and enter the fort over their dead bodies."

"That will not do!" broke in Heyward. "A soldier might force his way in this manner, but never with these ladies in the party."

"It would be a bloody path for them," admitted Hawkeye. "If we do not attack, we must turn aside and get outside the line of their guards. Then we can turn to the west and enter the mountains. I can hide you so that the devils in Montcalm's pay could not find you in months."

"Let us do that, and quickly!" said Heyward.

Hawkeye turned back over the path that had just brought them to this dangerous spot. They moved as quietly as possible, not knowing when they might meet another guard, and soon struck off toward the mountains to the west. The path led over broken ground, rough with rocks. Black hills rose on every side of them. Soon the path began to rise and wind among the rocks and trees, and the darkness began to thin out. Hawkeye led the way to an open space at the very top of an egg-shaped hill just as day broke, and they saw the sun above the green pines on the other side of the valley of the Horicon. The sisters got off their horses, and the horses were turned loose to find what food they could.

"Have we no more need for them?" asked Heyward.

"Judge for yourself," replied Hawkeye. "From up here, we can see into the heart of Montcalm's camp, but we can't tell what he will do."

◇◇

On the shore of the lake below them lay the low
buildings and earthworks of William Henry. The walls
swept down to the water on one side, while a deep
ditch ran around the other three sides. Around the fort
the woods had been cleared. Beyond that, the green of
the forest was broken at times by bare rocks. In the
front of the fort could be seen several guards, wearily
pacing back and forth. Inside the walls themselves the
little party looked down upon men still tired from a
night of watching. Toward the south and east, and
looking down on the fort from a rocky height, was
Montcalm's camp. It would have been much better if
the fort had been built on that height. A little farther
to the south smoke rose in several places, showing, as
Hawkeye pointed out, that the enemy lay in force in
that direction.

But the sight that most worried Heyward was on the
southwest bank of the lake. On a narrow strip of land
running from the Horicon to the foot of the mountain
were seen the white tents and heavy guns of a camp of
ten thousand men. Ground had already been thrown up
in front. And even as they were watching, the roar of
heavy guns rose and thundered along the hills.

"Morning," said the scout, "and the soldiers are being wakened with the guns. We are a few hours too late, for Montcalm has already filled the woods with his cursed Indians."

"Is there no way by which we might enter?" asked Heyward. "Being taken by the French would be better than falling into the hands of Indians."

"See!" exclaimed Hawkeye, pointing at Munro's quarters. "See how that shot made the stones fly from the Colonel's house! Those French will pull it down faster than it was put up."

"Duncan," said Cora, "I cannot bear the sight of this danger that I cannot share. Let us go to Montcalm and demand that he protect us."

"You can't get to him with your scalp," laughed Hawkeye. "If I had one of the thousand boats that lie along that shore, it could be done. Ha! the firing will soon stop, for a mist is closing in. Now, if you are equal to the work and will follow me, I'll make a push. I'd like to get down into that camp to scatter those Mingo dogs I see hiding in the bushes near the fort."

"We are ready for any danger," said Cora.

Hawkeye turned to her with a smile as he answered, "If I had a thousand men who feared death as little as you do, I'd send those lumbering French back within a

◇◇

week. But the mist is rolling in fast. We'll use it as cover. Remember, if anything happens to me, keep the air blowing on your left cheek—or rather, follow the Mohicans. They know their way, day or night."

Waving his hand for them to follow, he started down the hill, picking his way carefully. Heyward helped the girls, and in a few minutes they were far below on the side of a mountain they had climbed with so much pain. Soon they were on level ground about a half mile from a sally-port [5] on the west side of the fort. There they had to wait till the mist, now rolling down the lake, had hidden the camp of the enemy. The Mohicans took this time to look the ground over, and Hawkeye followed to learn his position. In a few minutes, however, he returned, talking to himself.

"Here that cunning Frenchman has posted sentinels right in our path—both Indians and whites, and we are as likely to fall into them as to pass them in this mist."

"Can't we circle them and find our path again?" asked Heyward.

As he was speaking, a thundering noise was heard and a cannon ball, entering the brush, bounded past them. The Indians followed it, and Hawkeye explained, "A

[5] *sally-port*, a gate at the side or rear of a fort.

small hope, but it's better than nothing. When other signs fail, we can pick up its path. Let's hurry, or the mist may leave us between the two armies—marks for both to shoot at."

Heyward placed himself between the two sisters to help them, but before they had gone twenty yards the fog had become so thick that they could hardly see each other. They made a little circle to the left and were coming back to the right, halfway to the fort, when close to them came a loud voice:

"Qui vive?"

"A friend of France," answered Heyward.

"Stop! or, by heaven, I'll make you a friend of the devil. Men, fire!"

The aim was bad, but the bullets whistled too close for comfort. The command came again, not only to fire, but to charge.

Hawkeye stopped and spoke firmly:

"We'll return the fire. They will think it is an attack and give way, or they will wait for help."

The plan was good, but it failed, and in a moment the whole plain was alive with men, their guns rattling from the shores of the lake far into the woods.

◇◇◇

"We shall draw their entire army upon us," said Heyward. "Lead on, friend, for your life and ours."

In the hurry of the moment, Hawkeye had lost his direction. He turned each cheek to get the wind, but each was equally cool. Then Uncas found the trail of the cannon ball where it had cut the ground through some ant hills.

"Give me the range!" said Hawkeye, bending to see the direction and then moving quickly forward.

There were cries, curses, voices calling to each other, and reports of guns on every side. Suddenly a strong light flashed across the plain, the fog rolled upward, and several cannon thundered, their echoes trembling in the hills.

"That is from the fort," exclaimed Hawkeye, turning short in his tracks, "and we are running to the woods, right into the knives of the Mohawks!"

The party turned around and ran in another direction, in danger every moment of being taken prisoners. Men, hot and angry, followed.

"Stand ready, my brave Sixtieths!" suddenly roared a voice directly above them. "Wait to see the enemy. Fire low and sweep the hill!"

"Father! Father!" screamed a high voice through the mist. "It's Alice! Save us!"

"Stop!" cried Munro's voice in perfect agony lest his daughters be hurt. "Throw open the gate! To the field, Sixtieths! Hold your fire and drive these French dogs back with your steel!"

Heyward heard the heavy gates open; then he saw a line of gallant men marching out and knew them for his Royal Americans. Now an officer ran forward, a man of huge frame and every inch a soldier, his hair white with years of service. With his arms around his daughters, the old Colonel turned to Heyward.

"Heyward, I knew you'd bring them to me safe."

"Thank you, sir," was Major Heyward's reply.

PART THREE

The massacre at Fort William Henry

CHAPTER 14

Heyward Meets Montcalm

◇◇◇

THE FEW days that followed were anxious days and full of danger. Munro had neither men nor means to hold out against Montcalm; and General Webb, with his army idle at Fort Edward, seemed to have forgotten the extreme need of his fellow Englishmen. Montcalm had filled the woods with Indians, whose yells chilled the hearts of all who heard them.

But inside the fort the men, following the example of their leaders, kept up their courage to an extent that gave pleasure to even so stern a man as Munro. Montcalm, as if satisfied with the hard march through the forests, had not gone on to seize the mountains from which he might much more easily have taken William

◇◇

Henry. Instead, he had planted his guns on the plains, but from there he used them with such wonderful skill that Munro could do little to defend his position.

It was on the fifth day of the attack. Major Heyward had stepped to the walls of the fort to get a breath of cool air from the lake. The evening was calm and the air fresh and mild. The roar of guns had stopped. The mountains, lighted by the setting sun, looked cool and lovely. Many islands dotted the lake, some low and some rounded like green hills.

Heyward stood looking out on the scene, when he saw a white flag coming toward the fort. Flags to cover the coming of messengers had appeared often, but this time, to his surprise, Heyward saw Hawkeye in the care of a French officer. Hawkeye looked tired and worn with care. His prized rifle was not with him. Indeed, his hands were tied behind him. The moment Heyward saw his friend, he turned and hurried toward Munro's quarters. But the sound of two voices caught his ear and he stopped to speak to Alice and Cora.

"Oh," said Alice, "for days—no, ages—we have been expecting you, but you have run away like a deer, as Hawkeye would say."

"Your father could tell you that although I have not seen you, I have still been thinking of your safety," returned the young man.

"Even so," said Cora in her quiet way, "we did wonder a little why you kept away from the place where Father could have expressed his thanks."

"Over there you see that village of huts?" asked Heyward. "The one who holds that is sure to hold the fort, too. I have been spending my days and my nights there because my duty demanded it, but I am deeply sorry if I seem to have neglected you."

"Duncan," said Alice, and a tear shone in her eye, "I hope this idle tongue of mine has not hurt you, for we are truly grateful for your help. Cora, especially, has spoken of it."

Heyward turned to her and noticed lines in her face. "Cora, I fear you are not well. We have joked while you were suffering."

"Look around you," she answered. "What joy can there be here for the daughter of a soldier whose greatest happiness is his honor?"

"Your father's honor cannot be stained by things which he cannot control. I am on my way to see him now. We shall meet again soon and I hope we shall then have driven the French away." He walked rapidly toward Munro's quarters.

Munro greeted him with: "I was about to send for you."

"I am sorry to see, sir, that the scout I praised so highly was taken by the French. I hope there is no reason for not trusting him."

"The loyalty of the Long Rifle is well known to me," replied Munro. "But his usual good fortune seems to have failed him. Montcalm made him a prisoner, and now, in his cursed gentlemanly way, has returned him with a note—'knowing how much you value him, I could not think of holding him longer'—his way of telling me of my change of fortune."

"Is Webb sending help?"

"Did you look to the south as you came? And did you see them?" asked the old soldier bitterly.

"But surely help will come!"

"I don't know. We have no word of when or by what path; but it seems there is a letter Montcalm took from Hawkeye. If the news were bad, the Frenchman would surely have told us."

"He keeps the letter while he returns the man," said Heyward. "We must decide quickly. We cannot hold the camp much longer—more than half the guns have burst."

"And why not? Some of them were fished from the bottom of the lake. Some have been going to pieces in the woods these many years. And we are three thousand miles away from England."

"The walls are breaking down and the supplies are giving out," said Heyward sadly. "Even the men show signs of worry and doubt."

"Major Heyward, I have served the King for fifty years, and I know the truth of what you say. Still, we owe much to the honor of the King's arms and something to ourselves. While there is any hope at all, I'll hold Fort William Henry, but we must see that letter to know what Webb will do."

"Can I be of service?"

"Sir, you can. Montcalm has asked me to meet him— to give me further information, he says. We must be as polite as he, but I do not want to let him think that we are worried. So I'll send you, since you are an officer of rank."

Heyward accepted the duty at once. He was soon ready, and, carrying a white flag, he and his little party went out to meet Montcalm.

◇◇◇

The General was surrounded by his officers and a band of Indian chiefs—among them, Sly Fox. A cry of surprise escaped Heyward, but he collected himself quickly.

Montcalm, in the flower of his age and in the height of his fortune, was well known for his courtly bearing and his courage. He had a fine smiling face and the noble air of a true soldier. And it was only two years later that, leading his men in person, he lost his life on the Plains of Abraham,[1] before Quebec.

"Sir," he said in French, "I find much pleasure in— but where is the officer to speak between us?"

"I do not think, sir, that one will be necessary. I speak French a little."

"Oh, I am very glad," said Montcalm, taking Heyward by the arm and leading him into his field tent. "I do not like those taletellers. One never knows where he stands with them. Well, sir, although I should have been proud to receive Colonel Munro, I am happy that he has sent a man as pleasing as yourself."

Heyward bowed low and Montcalm went on:

"Colonel Munro is a brave man and well able to com-

---

[1] *Plains of Abraham*, the level land high above the St. Lawrence River at Quebec. It was here that Montcalm later lost his life in a battle with the English army.

◇◇

mand his men. But, my dear sir, is it not time to think more of the lives in our charge and less of courage? One is as fine as the other."

"We think of the two as one," said Heyward, smiling.

"It is possible that my glasses have deceived me, and that your force stands off our guns better than I supposed. You know our strength?"

"We have heard different reports," said Heyward trying to speak carelessly. "The highest has not been more than twenty thousand men."

The Frenchman bit his lips and fixed his eyes on Heyward as if to read his thoughts. Then he continued, seeming to think well of this account that quite doubled his army:

"It does not speak well for the watchfulness of our soldiers that we cannot hide our numbers." After a moment he added, "The duties of a gentleman are not forgotten by one so young as yourself. I learn that the two daughters of Colonel Munro have passed into your fort."

"That is true, sir. But instead of weakening our efforts, they set us an example of courage. If courage alone would win a battle, I would trust the fort to the older of these daughters."

◇◇◇

"But even courage cannot do everything," said Montcalm. "I trust, sir, that you come with Munro's permission to treat for the surrender of Fort William Henry?"

"Does General Montcalm think our position so weak that we must give it up?"

"I should be sorry to have the defense continue so long as to stir up my red friends here." And Montcalm looked at a group of listening Indians. "I find it hard even now to hold them to our way of fighting."

Heyward made no answer, for he remembered painfully the dangers from which he and his friends had escaped only a few days ago.

"These gentlemen of the forest are most dangerous when held back," continued Montcalm. "It is not necessary to tell you how difficult it is to hold them. Shall we speak of terms?—Your fort is an earthwork and you have only twenty-three hundred men."

"But our fort defeated one French army," said Heyward, "and there is a strong force within a few hours' march, which we count as part of our means."

"Six or eight thousand men," said Montcalm coolly. "And their leader has wisely decided that they are safer in his fort than in the field."

Here Heyward bit his lip—Montcalm, he saw, was

not afraid of six or eight thousand men, and Heyward knew that Webb did not have that many. After a moment in thought, Montcalm took up the conversation as if it were Heyward's business to propose terms. Heyward, on the other hand, tried to show a confidence that would offset whatever Montcalm had learned in the letter taken from Hawkeye. Neither succeeded, and so Heyward took his leave. Although he carried away a good opinion of the courtly manner and wisdom of the enemy's leader, he had no opinion regarding the very thing he had come to learn. Montcalm followed him to the door of the tent, and again invited Munro to an early meeting. Heyward returned to William Henry and went at once to Munro's quarters.

CHAPTER 15

An Old Man's Honor

◇◇

MAJOR HEYWARD found Colonel Munro in his quarters with only his two daughters. The old gentleman and Alice were good-naturedly teasing each other, while Cora watched with that fondness which she always showed toward her younger sister. Not only the dangers through which they had passed but also those which they still had before them seemed to be forgotten in this happy family meeting. When Heyward came into the room the daughters greeted him and then, knowing that he had important business with their father, they excused themselves and left.

Munro, now alone with Heyward, paced the room for a few moments instead of asking the result of the meeting with Montcalm. Then he raised his eyes and exclaimed warmly, "They are a pair of excellent girls, Heyward."

"You well know my opinion of your daughters, Colonel Munro."

"True, true," said the father, in a troubled voice. "You were about to speak your mind the day you got here. But I thought an old soldier should not talk about a marriage where enemies of the King might be guests who were not invited. But I was wrong, Duncan."

"No matter how glad I am to hear this from you, sir, I have here a message from Montcalm."

"Let the Frenchman and all his army go to the devil, sir!" cried Munro. "He is not yet master of William Henry, nor will he ever be if Webb proves himself the man he should be. And Munro can still care for his family duties. Your mother, Duncan, was the child of my best friend. Your family has been an ornament to the name of Scotland."

Heyward noted that Munro took pleasure now in not thinking too much about Montcalm's message. But, knowing that the pleasure would be short, he let him enjoy it while he could.

◇◇

"My request, sir, went so far as to hope for the honor of being your son."

"Aye, boy, I understand you, but did you ask the girl?"

"On my honor, no!" said Heyward warmly.

"You are a gentleman, Heyward. But Cora Munro is a girl who needs not the advice and help of a father."

"Cora!"

"Yes—Cora. We are speaking of your feelings for Miss Munro, are we not?"

"I—I—I do not remember using her name. You have another child no less lovely."

"Alice?" exclaimed her father in surprise.

Heyward waited in silence. For several minutes Munro paced the room, thinking deeply. Then he spoke in a soft voice.

"You would be my son, Duncan. But do you know the history of the man you would call father? Sit down, young man."

By this time Montcalm was forgotten. Each drew up a chair, while the older man spent a few minutes in thought. At last he spoke:

"You know already, Major Heyward, that my family

was both old and honored. I was poor, and I wanted to marry Alice Graham, the only child of a lord of large estate. Her father would not consent, so I went into the service of the King. After I had shed much blood in different lands, duty took me to the West Indies. There I married a daughter of a gentleman of the islands, the woman who became the mother of Cora. On her mother's side, she came from the natives of the islands. To some people this seems a misfortune, but would *you* dare to scorn my child because of this?"

"God forbid!" exclaimed Heyward, "but it is the sweet and gentle nature of Alice that I love."

"Death took my wife," continued Munro, "and I returned to Scotland with my daughter. The dear girl I loved in Scotland had remained single twenty years, and now she took me for her husband."

"And became the mother of Alice?" asked Heyward eagerly.

"Yes," answered Munro. "And she lived but a year."

Munro sat thinking sadly of the past. Then he arose and, after taking a turn around the room, spoke again with the air of the soldier he was.

"Have you not word from Montcalm, Major Heyward?"

◇◇◇

Heyward delivered the message.

"So Montcalm wants to talk with me?" said **Munro.** "It might not be a bad plan to let him see that we can face him firmly in spite of his numbers."

"He seems sure of himself," replied Heyward.

"I wish he would visit our fort in open day, and with a storming party. That would be far better for us than the slow pounding he has chosen. The beauty and virtue of war have passed away. Our fathers followed no such cowardly plans."

"That may be true, but we must fight art with art. What is your pleasure in this matter?"

"I will meet the Frenchman at once. Go, Heyward; give them a roll of drums and send out a messenger to let him know who is coming. We will follow with a small guard—such respect is due to one who holds the honor of the King in his keeping."

Heyward hurried, as the day was fast coming to a close. A few minutes only were necessary to march out a few soldiers and to send out a flag. Heyward led the guard to the gate, where he found Munro ready, and they left the fort with their little party.

They had gone only a short distance when they saw the little army that attended Montcalm move forward.

The moment Munro caught sight of the white plume that waved in the hat of Montcalm, his eyes brightened and age no longer seemed to have any hold on his large and powerful body.

"Tell the boys to look well to their arms," he whispered to Heyward, "for one is never safe with an officer of the French king. At the same time we must make him think that we feel sure of ourselves."

There was a roll of a drum from the French side; it was answered by the English and each party advanced. The careful Munro stopped with his guard close by. Montcalm moved forward with a quick, graceful step, baring his head and sweeping his white plume nearly to the earth as he bowed. Then he, being the superior officer, spoke first.

"I am happy, sir," he said to Heyward, "that you have again given us the pleasure of your company."

Heyward looked around him as he bowed. He was not at all at ease, for he saw many groups of Indians looking out from the woods, curiously watching the meeting.

"General Montcalm will note the difference in our positions," he said, pointing toward the red men. "Were we to let our guards go, we should stand here at the mercy of our enemies."

◇◇◇

"Sir," returned Montcalm, "you have the promise of a French gentleman for your safety. That should be enough."

"It shall." Heyward turned to the officer who led the guard. "Fall back, sir, beyond hearing, and wait for orders."

Montcalm drew nearer and opened the meeting.

"I have asked for this meeting, sir," he said, speaking to Heyward, "because I believe that Colonel Munro has done everything possible for the honor of his king, and will now be guided by pity for those under him. His defense has been brave, but there is no longer hope."

Heyward turned to Munro, and repeated Montcalm's words in English. The Colonel then replied:

"However much I may prize this word from General Montcalm, it will mean more to me when I have earned it."

Montcalm smiled, then continued:

"What I would freely give because of your courage, I might refuse because of stubborn holding out. Would you wish to see for yourselves my camp and the numbers of our men? That would show you how useless it would be to try to fight us."

"I know that the King of France is well served," re-

plied Munro, "but my own royal master has as many and as faithful troops."

"Though not at hand now, and that is well for us," said Montcalm.

"Ask the French general if his glasses can reach to the Hudson," said Munro proudly, "and if he knows when and where to expect the army of Webb."

"Let Webb answer," said Montcalm, and he handed Munro an open letter.

As Munro read, his face changed, his lip trembled, and the paper fell from his hand. Heyward caught the letter and, without saying anything, read it. General

◇◇◇

Webb urged them to give up the fort, and in plain terms said that he could not send a single man to save them.

"This is Webb's own handwriting," said Munro, bitterly. "He has brought dishonor to one who has never known it before, and heaped shame on my gray hairs."

"We are still masters of the fort and of our honor!" cried Heyward. "Let us sell our lives at such a rate as will make the enemy believe it too dear!"

"Boy, I thank thee," said Munro, "for you have reminded me of my duty. We will go back and dig our own graves inside our own fort."

"Gentlemen," said Montcalm with true interest, "Montcalm does not mean to use this letter to shame brave men. Listen to my terms before you leave.—To hold the fort is not possible. In the interest of my master, the King of France, it must be destroyed. But, as for you and your brave men, you shall be allowed every honor due to a soldier."

"Our colors?" asked Heyward.

"Carry them to England and show them to your king."

"Our arms?"

"Keep them. None can use them better."

"Our march from the fort? Our property?"

◇◇

"All shall be done in a way most honorable to you."

Heyward explained these terms to Munro, who was deeply touched by Montcalm's generous offer.

"Go, Duncan," said Munro, "with the General to his field tent and arrange it all. I have lived to see in my old age two things I had never expected: an Englishman afraid to help a friend, and a Frenchman too honest to profit by his advantage."

Then Munro returned to the fort, showing by his sadness that he was bringing bad news, and from this blow the old man never recovered.

Heyward returned late at night with the terms that Montcalm had laid down for the giving over of the fort. The English soldiers were to leave early in the morning. They were to keep their arms, their colors, their baggage, and their honor. Munro signed the papers and the fighting stopped at once.

CHAPTER 16

A Heartless Attack

◇◇◇

THE ARMIES of Montcalm lay in the wilds of Horicon on the night of August 9, 1757. Morning was drawing near. The stillness of the forest was broken now and then by a gay call of some French soldier on the early watch, or by a call from the fort into which no Frenchman could step before the time agreed upon.

Montcalm was awake early, for he was worried. The Indians had been hard to control in war—could he control them in peace? Shaking off his fear, he gave the order for the signal that would awaken the army. The first tap of the drums rang through the forest and soon the valley was filled with strains of military music. The horns of the French were loud and merry. The fifes of the English sounded once, and then were silent. Montcalm's plans for taking over the English fort were given out, and the company chosen to guard the gates marched before their chief.

Within the fort, the English and Americans made ready for a hurried march. With heavy hearts the soldiers shouldered their empty guns and fell into their places, trying to hide even from each other the hurt that all of them felt. Women and children ran from place to place, some carrying baggage, some looking for the husbands or fathers who would protect them.

Munro appeared among his men, firm and unhappy. This blow, so little expected, had struck far into his heart. Heyward, touched at his deep grief, stepped to Munro's side to offer help.

"My daughters," was Munro's brief, sad reply.

"Good heavens!" cried Heyward. "Have not plans been made for their safety?"

"Today I am only a soldier, Major Heyward," said the old man. "All here are my children who ask me to protect them."

Heyward hurried to Munro's quarters, where he found the sisters ready to go. Cora looked pale and worried, but she had lost none of her spirit. Alice had been weeping. Both received Heyward with open pleasure.

◇◇

"The fort is lost," said Cora, with a sad smile, "but our good name remains, I hope."

"It is brighter than ever," replied Heyward. "And now you will have time to think less of others and to give some thought to yourself. Military rule demands that your father and I march for a little time with the men, but we must find protection for you."

"None is necessary," returned Cora. "Who would dare to harm the daughters of such a father at a time like this?"

"If it were possible for me to stay with you, I would not leave you for the best office in the pay of the King— but look to Alice. She is suffering because she does not have your firmness."

"Listen!" said Cora. "Chance sends us a friend."

Hearing sounds of sacred music, Heyward knew that David was near and, indeed, David came. Heyward explained his wishes.

"I will attend to the young ladies when I have sung my morning praise," replied David. "Will you join me, friend, in singing 'Southwell'?" [1]

Then, taking the pitch, David sang his song. When it was finished, Heyward continued:

[1] *Southwell,* a hymn sung to a tune written by Southwell.

"It will be your duty to care for these daughters of Colonel Munro. Let no one harm them or speak ill of their brave father. If anyone troubles them, report him to Montcalm. A word will be enough."

"If not, I have here what will," returned David, showing his book. "Here are words to quiet the most stormy tempers."

Heyward assured the sisters that he had done the best he could for them and, as he believed, quite enough for their safety. He then said that, as soon as the army had gone a few miles toward the Hudson, he would return to them.

The order for marching was given; the English lines began to move. The sisters started at the sound and, as a great cloud seemed to pass over them, they looked up to see that they were standing under the folds of the French flag.

"Let us go," said Cora. "This is no longer a fit place for the daughters of an English officer."

Alice held tightly to Cora's arm and together they left, moving with the mass of people. As they passed the gates, the French officers, having learned who the girls were, bowed low and often. Since every horse and

wagon had been used to carry the sick and wounded,
the girls walked. The whole group was now on the way:
the men in angry silence, the women in terror of they
knew not what.

Montcalm now held Fort William Henry. Three
thousand English moved together toward the road
through the forest and toward Fort Edward on the
Hudson. Along the edge of the woods hung dark clouds
of Indians eying their late enemies like hawks, ready to
dive down on them at a moment's notice. A few Indians
had mixed with the marchers.

The first soldiers, with Heyward at their head, had
already reached the woods when Cora's attention was
drawn to a group at the end of the line. One of the soldiers had left his place in the line because an Indian was
trying to take from him the baggage he carried. He was
a large, strong man and would not easily give up his
property. Other men from both sides took part, either
to prevent or to aid the robbery.

Voices grew loud and angry, and a hundred Indians
appeared where only a dozen had been a minute before.
It was then that Cora saw Sly Fox moving among the
red men and speaking to them. The women and chil-

dren stopped and drew together like frightened birds. But the greed of the Indians was soon satisfied, and the line moved slowly on.

The Indians now fell back and seemed willing to let their enemies march away without troubling them further. But as one woman passed by, the bright colors of her baby's blanket caught the eyes of a Huron, who seized both the blanket and the child. The woman ran after him to get back her baby. The Indian, laughing cruelly, caught the blanket in one hand and, with the other hand, caught the baby by the feet and swung it above his head.

"Take anything!" the woman screamed, "but give me my baby!"

The savage now saw that another Indian had got the prize he wanted. Angered at this, he dashed the head of the baby against a rock and threw the dead body at the mother's feet. Then, maddened at the sight of the blood, he drove his tomahawk into the mother's brain.

At this moment, Sly Fox put his hands to his mouth and gave the terrible Indian war whoop. The Indians started at the well-known cry. Then along the plain

there arose a yell that rang through the woods till all of Munro's army listened with terror in their hearts.

With that cry, more than two thousand savages broke from the forest and rushed among the people in the line, striking them down with blows from their tomahawks. According to the terms of surrender, the guns of Munro's men were not loaded. So, hoping to satisfy the Indians, some of the men let the savages tear the guns from their hands. Others of the soldiers threw themselves into masses, trying to frighten the Hurons by a military front. But the wounded and sick were killed and scalped in cold blood.

For some minutes the frightened sisters stood looking on. Their father was the highest officer among the English—would they not be safe? And so thought others. Screaming women and children pressed around the girls, making escape impossible. Alice caught sight of her father walking back toward the French army. He was going to Montcalm. Many axes threatened his life, but even in their rage, the Indians respected his rank and his calmness. Munro brushed them aside and marched on.

"Father! Father! We are here!" cried Alice, but in

◇◇

the noise he could not hear her call. Alice dropped in a faint and Cora stooped over to protect her.

"Lady, this is the holiday of the devils and not a fit place for Christians!" said the voice of David. "Let us fly!"

"Go and save yourself!" said Cora. "You cannot help us now," and she bent again over Alice.

Seeing this strength of will, and being a man of firm faith, David drew himself up to his full height. "It may be that I can tame the spirits of these devils with song," he said and, raising his voice to its highest pitch, he poured out a song that was heard even above the noise of that bloody field. More than one Huron had rushed toward the sisters thinking to get some colored pieces of their dresses or to carry away their scalps. But this song made them stop and listen—then they passed on to other and less brave victims. David's song caught the ear of Sly Fox, who flew raging from group to group. When he saw the sisters again at his mercy, he gave a yell of triumph.

"Come," he said, laying his bloody hand on Cora's arm. "The wigwam of the Huron is still open. Is it not better than this?" Then, with a laugh full of scorn, he held up his hand and continued, "It is red, but it comes from white hearts."

"Beast!" cried Cora. "It was you who brought this murder on my people!"

"The Fox is a great chief! Will the dark-hair go with him?"

"Never! I should far rather be killed!"

The Fox stopped for a moment, then caught the light form of Alice up from the ground and started swiftly toward the woods.

"Let her go!" screamed Cora, running wildly after him. But the Fox knew his power and would hold it, for Cora would go wherever he carried Alice. David followed and across the plain they ran, past the wounded and the dead. The Fox, knowing the woods well, entered through a low pass where he had tied the horses he had taken from the white party a few days before. There another Indian was waiting, as fierce and cruel as the Fox himself. They motioned to Cora to mount one of the horses. She did so, then held out her arms toward Alice with a look of such pleading that even the Fox was touched, and put the senseless form in Cora's arms. The Fox then seized the lead strap and plunged

◇◇◇

into the forest. David threw his long leg over another horse and followed.

Soon they began to climb into hills, and Alice began to come to herself. They could hear the awful cries from the plain below, but the minds of the sisters were too full of fear to notice the path they were taking. When they gained the flat top of the mountain, however, Cora saw it was the same spot to which she had been led before by Hawkeye. Now from this place, where the Fox let them off the horses, they could look down on the terrible sight below. The murder continued until the Indians' thirst for revenge had been satisfied. But at length it ended, the cries died out, and all was again quiet.

CHAPTER 17

Again in the Hands of the Enemy

◊◊◊

THREE days after the fall of Fort William Henry, the shores of Horicon were as still as death. The French had gone and left the fort a smoking ruin. The weather, too, had changed. The sun was hidden behind heavy mists. The smooth mirror of the lake was gone, and now green and angry waves covered it and pounded the shores. The whole country that had looked so lovely was now clouded by a heavy sheet of driving fog.

As the sun was setting, five men came from a cover of trees and, watching closely, moved toward the ruins. One of them, an Indian, moved a little to one side and watched the edge of the woods with eyes trained to see the smallest signs. A light figure went ahead of the oth-

◇◇◇

ers, passing the groups of dead, searching among all of the still bodies. Another of the group, whose gray locks and military step showed him to be an old soldier, often groaned aloud at the terrible picture before him. The look of pain on his face showed how deeply he hated a crime like this. He was a father in search of his children. The fifth man was seeking someone whom he had learned to love.

Uncas, who had now reached the center of the plain, raised a cry that drew the others to him. Before him lay a mass of bodies. The scout, Hawkeye, spoke:

"I have been on many a sad field, and have followed a trail of blood for many miles, but never have I seen the devil so plain as here. Revenge is an Indian's desire, and I am white, but this I say: as long as guns will fire and fire will burn, these French had better not trust themselves within range of my rifle. What do you say, Great Serpent? Shall the Hurons boast of this to their women when deep snows come?"

An angry look flashed across the face of the Mohican chief as he touched the knife at his belt. Uncas, who had been searching in the ruins, suddenly bounded away. He returned in a moment waving a piece of red riding veil.

"My child!" cried Munro. "Give me my child!"

"Uncas will try," was the touching answer.

"Either she or those that have robbed her have passed this bush," said Hawkeye. "The dark-hair was here. Let us search for other marks. I sometimes think Indian eyes can follow the track of a bird."

Uncas pushed ahead and at once raised a shout of success. On a low branch of a tree he had found another bit of the veil.

"My good man," said Munro to Hawkeye, "where have they gone?"

"If they are alone, they are quite likely to move in a circle and may be near us now. If the Hurons have them, they may be near Canada. But the Mohicans and I are on one end of the trail, and we'll find them if they are a hundred miles away."

"Hugh!" exclaimed Great Serpent, who was examining the bushes. He stood up and pointed down at the ground, like a man who has seen a stinging snake.

"Here is the mark of a man's foot," said Heyward. "The girls have been taken prisoners."

"Better to be prisoners than to starve in these woods," said Hawkeye. "I'll bet fifty beaver skins against as many guns that the Mohicans and I enter their wigwams within this moon. Look, Uncas, and see what you can make of the moccasin, for plainly it is no shoe."

Uncas stooped and examined the leaves as closely as a money dealer would examine a bank note. At length he arose. "Sly Fox," he said.

"That devil again?" cried Hawkeye. "There will be no end to this till my Killdeer has spoken to him."

Heyward felt less sure. "One moccasin is so much like another," he said. "There might be a mistake."

"One moccasin like another!" retorted Hawkeye. "You might as well say one foot is just like another. Some feet are long and some are short. Some are wide and some are narrow. Some toe in and some toe out. One moccasin is no more like another than one book is like another—to anyone who can read them."

He bent down to look more closely.

"You are right, boy. And the fellow drinks firewater. Your drinking Indian walks with his feet wide apart. The Fox and the dark-hair have passed here."

"And not Alice?" asked Heyward.

"We have no signs of her yet," returned Hawkeye, but he continued to examine the trees, the bushes, and the ground. "Ah! Uncas, bring what you see hanging from that bush."

When the scout received the prize, he held it up and laughed heartily.

"It's that tooting thing the singer carries," he said. "Uncas, look for the marks of a shoe big enough to hold up the six feet two of that fellow. He has given up singing to follow a better trade."

"At least he has been faithful to his trust," said Heyward, "and Cora and Alice have a friend with them. But let us begin our march. A moment to them will seem like an age."

"It's not the swiftest deer that gives the longest chase," returned Hawkeye. "We know that the Hurons have passed here, and the lady, and the singer. We'll push farther and if we find no signs of the yellow locks, we must come back and look for more signs. Uncas, keep your eyes on the dry leaves. I'll watch the bushes while your father runs with a low nose to the ground."

"Is there nothing I can do?" asked Heyward.

"Yes!" replied Hawkeye. "Stay behind us, and don't cross the trail!"

They had gone only a little way when the Indians stopped, speaking in excited voices to each other. Hawkeye hurried up.

"They have found the print of a little foot!" he

exclaimed. "And what have we here? By the best gun in the land, here have been them one-sided horses again! Now all is as plain as the north star. Here the horses were tied to a tree, and here they mounted. Their path leads north, toward Canada."

"And still no sign of Alice?" asked Heyward.

"Unless something Uncas has just picked up off the ground is hers. Let us see."

It was a piece of jewelry that Alice had worn. Eagerly Heyward suggested:

"We should not wait longer. Let us start our march at once."

"Young blood and hot blood are much the same," said Hawkeye. "This is no squirrel hunt that we are starting—it's a long, hard hunt. We'll have to lie out for days and nights, and stretch across woods where no book learning could carry you. An Indian never starts on such a hunt without smoking over his council fire, and in that he is right. We'll go back, light our fire to-night in the old fort, and in the morning we'll be fresh to start out like men."

Heyward knew he could not shake Hawkeye from this purpose, and so he took Munro by the arm and followed the Indians and the scout back across the plain.

CHAPTER 18

Ghosts in the Night

◇◇

EVENING had come when the party entered the ruins of Fort William Henry and prepared to spend the night there. Hawkeye and the Indians lighted their fire and took their simple meal of dried bear meat, while Heyward walked over to that part of the fort that had looked out upon the waters of the Horicon. The wind had fallen and the waves were now rolling more evenly on the sandy beach. The heavy clouds, as if tired of their day's chase, were gathering in dark masses low in the sky, while lighter ones touched the tops of the mountains like birds in flight. Here and there a star struggled through the low clouds, throwing its red light over the heavens. Within the circle of the hills, a heavy darkness had settled and the plain lay like a great death house without a whisper to waken the unhappy people who slept there.

Heyward stood for many minutes looking out upon this scene. He fancied that he could hear sounds, perhaps voices. Thinking he heard footsteps, he returned and spoke in a low voice to Hawkeye, who threw his rifle across his arm and then stood very still, listening. Hearing nothing, he spoke:

"An Indian seldom sleeps in war, and one of the Hurons might have remained to steal, although an Indian almost never hangs around graves. After the spirit is gone, he is usually willing to let the dead rest. Speaking of spirits, Major, do you think the redskins and the whites have the same heaven?"

"No doubt," returned Heyward, "but I thought I heard it again."

"I believe," said Hawkeye, "that everybody will be happy in heaven according to his own likes and gifts, and that the Indian is not far wrong when he looks ahead to the happy hunting grounds."

"Did you hear it again?" asked Heyward.

"Maybe a wolf," said Hawkeye. "They are bold when they are hungry. You know, Major, I've heard it said that heaven is a place to rest. For one who has always lived in the woods and who loves to hunt, that wouldn't be easy, but it would be a change.—Listen—what goes there?"

He moved into the shadow and Heyward followed.

"We must call Uncas," said the scout. "The boy has Indian senses and may hear what we can't."

Uncas, who had been speaking to his father, started to his feet as he heard the call of an owl. The scout repeated the call, and in a few minutes Uncas came stealing along the wall toward him. As soon as Hawkeye had told the reason for his call, Uncas threw himself flat on the ground, where he appeared to lie perfectly still. After some moments had passed, Heyward took a few steps toward where he had been, but Uncas was gone.

"What has become of him?" exclaimed Heyward under his breath. "I saw him drop there, and I would have sworn he was still there."

"Speak lower," said Hawkeye. "You don't know what ears are open, but Uncas is out there on the plain and if any Mingoes are there they will find their equal."

"Let's give the alarm to the others and get our guns; there are five of us," urged Heyward.

"I'll tell Great Serpent we are after a Mingo," said Hawkeye. "His Indian nature will tell him what to do."

Hawkeye put his fingers to his mouth and made a low hissing sound like a snake. Although Great Serpent's dark eyes looked swiftly on every side when he heard this sound of the animal whose name he bore, he arose slowly. He made no move toward his rifle. The tomahawk that he had loosened in his belt fell to the ground. Then he sat down again by the fire as calmly as only an Indian could. He appeared to go to sleep, but his head was turned a little so that he might hear the better, and his eye took in everything.

"A brave Indian!" exclaimed Hawkeye. "He knows that a look or a move might put us all at the mercy of those devils."

There was a flash and the roar of a rifle. Sparks flew into the air near Great Serpent, and he disappeared. Soon there was a plunge in the water, then another report of a gun.

"There goes Uncas!" said Hawkeye. "That boy carries a smart gun. I know its crack as a father knows the sound of his child's voice, for it was mine until I got a better one."

"They have found us, and we are marked for death!" said Heyward.

Great Serpent returned to the circle of the light.

"How is it?" asked Hawkeye. "Are there many Mingoes near? Or is there just one snake hanging around?"

The chief quietly took his seat. He looked closely to the spot where the bullet had struck just above his head, and then, holding up a single finger, he said:

"One."

"I thought so," said Hawkeye, "and now the devil will tell his lies of how he trailed Mohicans and a white scout. Well, let him—let him."

Uncas slipped into the light and seated himself as calmly as his father. This was not the moment for a Mohican to boast. And perhaps, without Heyward's question, nothing more would have been said of the matter.

"What has become of your enemy, Uncas? We heard you fire."

The young chief lifted a fold of his hunting shirt and brought forth a scalp. There had been one enemy near; Uncas had brought in one scalp. Uncas and his father knew they were safe, but Heyward, feeling less sure of himself, returned to the ruins of the fort.

Great Serpent, sitting before the fire, lighted a pipe, whose bowl was curiously carved from the soft stone of the country. He smoked a moment, then passed the pipe over to the scout. Three times the pipe passed between them before either spoke. Then Great Serpent began to speak in the Mohican tongue. He was answered by Hawkeye. Comments and answers continued, but, in his respect for the older men, Uncas said nothing until Hawkeye asked his opinion.

Heyward knew they were trying to decide upon the best way to travel in their search for the prisoners. Uncas and his father wanted to go by land. Hawkeye wanted to go on the lake. The argument grew warm until at last Hawkeye carried his point and the Mohicans accepted his plan with a friendly air that proved Hawkeye had really changed their minds.

Hawkeye stretched his long body before the dying fire, and soon was asleep. Great Serpent wrapped his head in his blanket and stretched himself on the bare

earth. Uncas heaped the coals so that they would warm
his father's feet. Then Uncas looked for a comfortable
place among the ruins. And long before the night had
turned, these five, who lay within what had been the
old fort, slept as soundly as those who lay outside.

PART FOUR

In the camp
of the enemy

CHAPTER 19

The Chase Up the Lake

THE HEAVENS still shone with stars when Hawkeye awoke the party. Munro and Heyward were on their feet in a moment waiting for orders.

"Think over your prayers, but don't speak a word," said the scout. "He who hears them knows the language of the heart as well as that of the tongue, and few white voices are pitched right for the woods. Come," he continued, turning to leave the fort, "get into the ditch on this side. Step on stones and on pieces of wood as you go. Marks are easily left in grass, but wood and stone take no print from a moccasin. Push the canoe in close to the land, Uncas, but carefully—it must not touch the beach, or the devils will know by what way we have left."

Hawkeye, laying a board from the ruins to the canoe, made a sign for the two officers to cross over. Then Hawkeye covered all footprints and other marks left by the party and stepped into the canoe. Silently the paddles pushed them ahead till the ruins of William Henry were far behind.

"There is much water between them and us now, and they can't track us," said the scout. "We shall have the length of the Horicon behind us before our enemies have made up their minds which way to take."

"With enemies all around, our journey will be a dangerous one," said Heyward.

"Danger?" repeated Hawkeye. "Not exactly, for we can keep a few hours ahead of the varlets. And if we must use the guns, three of us can use them as well as any in the land. We probably have a hard journey ahead of us and perhaps a fight, but we can find cover and powder is plenty."

Heyward now sat in silence as the canoe shot over several miles of water. Just as day broke, they entered the narrows of the lake and stole with great care among the many islands. Montcalm had gone back by this way, and he might have left some Indians to protect his rear forces. The Great Serpent laid aside his paddle and looked carefully from one island to another. By a light tap on the side of the canoe he signaled that danger was near.

"What now?" asked Hawkeye. "The lake is smooth, and I can see along its sheet for miles."

The Indian raised his hand and pointed. Heyward could see nothing but mist that rose from the water. The scout saw that and also an edge of black smoke which, he said, came from a dying fire.

"The party must be small if it can lie on such a small island," said Heyward. "Let us hurry on."

"You can't judge Indian cunning by the rules you find in books," said Hawkeye, looking more closely. "We must choose between two things: return and give up all thought of following the Hurons——"

"Never!" cried Heyward.

"Well, I am much of that mind myself," continued Hawkeye. "Then we must make a push, and if the Indians or French are in the narrows, run the gauntlet [1] through these islands. Is there reason in my words, Great Serpent?"

---

[1] *gauntlet.* Usually a gauntlet was made up of two lines of men armed with clubs or knives. A captive was made to run between the lines while the men struck at him. Here Hawkeye and his party must try to run through the lanes of islands and enemy canoes.

For answer the Indian dropped his paddle into the water and pushed the canoe forward. In a few moments they could see the north shore of the island and there they saw, too, other Indians—"Two canoes and a smoke," said Hawkeye. A shot from the island, followed by a wild yell, told that the English party had been seen. The Hurons rushed to their canoes and took up the chase.

"Keep this distance between them and us," said Hawkeye. "They have no guns that will reach us, but my Killdeer has a barrel on which any man can depend."

Three times Hawkeye raised the gun to his shoulder; three times he waited for the enemy to come nearer. As he seemed ready at last to fire, a low cry from Uncas stopped him. Uncas had spotted another war canoe pushing across their course, a little way in front of them! The scout put down his gun and took up his paddle, and now, indeed, they pulled for dear life. The Hurons were not more than two hundred yards away, and pressing forward with wild shouts.

Now if the scout and his party were to save themselves, they must trust to speed alone. Both their canoe and the canoes of the Hurons plunged forward so fast

that the waves curled in white foam from their bows.
The Hurons were so busy at the paddles that they had
not as yet tried to shoot. But Hawkeye and the Mohicans were growing tired and the Hurons had more
men to carry them on. Hawkeye looked back anxiously.

"Edge her a little more away from the sun," he said.
"One of the Hurons has picked up his gun, and a single
mistake might lose us our scalps. Edge over, and we'll
put the island between us."

This they did, then all doubled their efforts, coming
around the last low point like racers, with the Mohicans
still in the lead.

"They are going to shoot!" exclaimed Heyward.
"And we are right in line with them. They can hardly
miss!"

"Get down into the bottom of the canoe, you and the
Colonel."

"Not while others are under fire," said Heyward.

A burst of shots, and the whistling of bullets around
them stopped their talking for a moment.

"Now that is real courage!" said Hawkeye to Heyward. Uncas looked surprised at the young officer's willingness to meet the danger which he might have escaped. But Great Serpent, having seen courage before in his white friends, merely kept his eyes on the object by which he was guiding their course. A bullet struck Great Serpent's paddle and knocked it out of his hand, but he caught it up out of the water, waved it high over his head, and gave the war whoop of the Mohicans.

From the canoes behind there were cries of "Great Serpent!" "The Long Rifle!" "Bounding Elk!" Hawkeye seized his gun, held it high, and shook it at his enemies. The Hurons answered with another yell and a round of shots. The bullets scattered along the lake, and one even made a hole in the bark of the little canoe. In all this exciting chase, the faces of the Mohicans showed neither hope nor alarm. The scout, turning his head, laughed in his own quiet way and said to Heyward, "The Mingoes love to hear the sound of their

own guns, but not one of them can shoot straight in a
dancing canoe. And even now we go ahead three feet to
their two."

The scout now gave his paddle to Heyward so that he
might, as he said, "let Killdeer play his part." He stead-
ied himself and took aim. At the same time, the Huron
in the bow of the leading canoe rose to draw on the
scout. But before he could fire, Killdeer spat out his bit
of lead, and the Huron fell, his rifle dropping from his
hand into the water.

Now the canoes that were chasing pulled together
and stopped. The Mohican and his son eased up a moment for breath, each looking to see if the other had
been hurt, for each well knew that no cry of pain would
be allowed to escape the other. A few large drops of
blood were dripping from the shoulder of the Great
Serpent. He dipped some water in his hand and washed
them off.

"Softly," said Hawkeye as he loaded again. "The
devils are holding council. Let them come within striking distance, and with Killdeer I'll take a life twice out
of three trials."

"We forget our errand," said Heyward. "With God's
help, let us hurry."

◇◇◇

Obeying the officer, Hawkeye laid down his gun and took up a paddle. But instead of following the west shore, the Mohican turned toward the hills farther east, where Montcalm was known to have led his army into the strong fort of Ticonderoga.[2]

The Hurons seemed to have given up the chase, but for hours the Mohicans drove the canoe on till they reached a bay near the north end of the lake. Then Hawkeye and Heyward climbed a hill near by and looked out over the water. In a moment the scout pointed to a dark object several miles back.

"What would you take that to be?" he asked.

"A bird, or perhaps a rock," replied Heyward.

"It's a canoe, and it is full of fierce Mingoes. The dear Lord gave good eyes to men who live in the woods— better than to those who live in towns and have glasses to help their sight. Those Mingoes pretend to be getting their evening meal, but they will be on our trail the moment it is dark. We'll have to throw them off if we want to find that Sly Fox."

They pulled over to the shore, lifted the canoe from the water, and carried it on their shoulders, leaving a broad trail. They crossed a stream and continued till

---

[2] *Ticonderoga*, a fort at the north end of Lake George.

they reached a large, bare rock where they would leave no footprints. Then they returned to the stream, but on the way back they very carefully walked backwards. Following the bed of the stream back to the lake, they again set the canoe in the water. Under cover of low branches, and soon hidden by the darkness, they pushed quietly back toward the west shore. Like the experienced man he was, the Mohican knew a good landing spot. The canoe was lifted and carried into the woods, where it was hidden under a pile of brush. Then, picking up their arms and packs, they set out on foot.

CHAPTER 20

Finding the Huron's Trail

◇◇

THE PARTY had reached that high land which separates the waters flowing into Lake Champlain from those flowing into the Hudson and Mohawk rivers. Towns have since been built near there, but even now no one but the hunter or the Indian is ever known to enter its deepest hiding places. Hawkeye and the Mohicans did not hesitate, however. They plunged in, and, after traveling for hours, guided by a star or following some stream, Hawkeye stopped the party. They built a fire and lay down to sleep for the rest of the night. Heyward and Munro, too, slept soundly.

When the sun had cleared the mist from the valley, the party arose and continued the journey. Hawkeye and the chief talked together often, and often stopped to look for any possible sign of the prisoners. During one of these talks, Uncas stood quiet as always, respecting the older men, but with a look of unusual interest on his face. Seeing this, his father asked the reason. Running ahead like a deer, Uncas pointed to a mark in a soft spot of earth.

"It's the trail!" exclaimed Hawkeye.

"See!" cried Uncas, "The dark-hair has been here!"

This success, after many miles of circling about, gave new hope to the party and they went on rapidly. If a rock or a bit of earth broke the path, the true eye of Hawkeye picked it up even at a distance.

By the middle of the afternoon they reached a low bottom where a stream flowed. There they discovered where the party of Sly Fox had made a stop. Although footsteps of man and beast were plainly seen, the trail seemed to end suddenly and the horses to have wandered without riders. At length Uncas, who had set out to find what path the horses had taken, came back leading them. Their saddles were broken as though they had run at will for several days.

"What should this tell?" asked Heyward, turning pale.

◇◇◇

"That we are in the enemy's country," replied the
scout. "If the Fox had been pressed, he might have
killed the girls. But with no enemy at his heels, he
wouldn't harm a hair of their heads, for not even a
Mingo would ill-treat a woman, unless to tomahawk
her.—But the Hurons have gone away on foot, and
we'll have to hunt carefully to find their path."

They began at the spring and went over the ground
by inches. They looked at every leaf. They moved sticks
and lifted stones, for Indian cunning knew well how to
hide every footstep. At last Uncas, searching the earth
along the little stream that ran from the spring, found
the print of a moccasin.

"The lad will be an honor to his people," said Hawkeye. "Yes, and a thorn in the side of the Hurons. Yet
that is not the mark of an Indian's foot. The weight is
too much on the heel, and the toes are square. Run
back, Uncas, and bring me the size of the singer's foot.
There's a beautiful print beside that rock over there."

The mark was, indeed, the size of David's large foot.
They now knew that David had been made to trade his
shoes for moccasins.

"I can read it now," said Hawkeye. "The singer was
made to go first. The others have walked in his steps."

"But," cried Heyward, "I see no signs of——"

"The maidens," said Hawkeye. "The Fox has found a way to throw us off the scent, but we'll find their little feet again."

The whole party went ahead now, following the bed of a small stream. For more than a half mile they went, until, on a bed of moss, Uncas found the mark of a foot. Following its direction, he struck the trail again.

"It was planned with real Indian judgment," said Hawkeye, "and would have fooled white eyes. It's all plain but one thing: how did they get the women along the blind trail? Even a Huron would be too proud to let their feet touch the water."

"Will this help explain the difficulty?" said Heyward, pointing beside the trail to a stretcher [1] made of rough poles, tied together with willow twigs.

"I see now!" cried Hawkeye. "They carried the maidens on that stretcher. Them varlets have spent hours trying to hide their trail. I've known them to spend days to the same purpose. Here are three pairs of moccasins and two little feet. By the Lord! Tall and lovely maidens they are, and yet such small feet!"

[1] *stretcher*, a kind of bed for carrying a sick or wounded person.

◇◇

"My daughters are not used to such hard walking," said Munro. "They will be completely worn out."

"Oh, don't you fear," returned the scout. "This is a firm, light step. The heel has hardly touched the ground. And there the dark-hair has made a little jump from one root to another. At this point neither of them was tired.—Now here the singer's legs were beginning to weaken. Here he slipped; there he traveled wide. And there it looks as if he had walked on snowshoes. Aye, a man who uses his throat so much can't train his legs properly."

Hawkeye's reasons were so clear that the whole party was cheered. They made a short stop to eat a meal. That ended, the scout looked at the setting sun and pushed on with such speed that the others found it hard to keep up with him. The trail was clear and open now and could be seen easily. From the valley Hawkeye began looking from side to side, but soon he stopped and waited for his party.

"The camp of the Hurons is near," he said to the Mohicans. "Great Serpent, you take the hillside to the right. Uncas, you go along the brook to the left. I'll try the trail. If anything happens, the sign will be three calls of the crow. I saw a crow fanning himself in the air—another sign that we are near a camp."

As Heyward was anxious to get a look at the enemy, the scout told him to steal to the edge of the wood and wait there. Looking through the bushes, he saw that many trees had been felled, and, at some distance from him, the stream had widened into a lake. The work seemed to have been done by the hands of men. A hundred rude huts stood on the edge of the lake, their round roofs shaped for protection against the weather. In fact, the whole village seemed better planned and more neat than most Indian villages. Heyward fancied that several people were coming toward him on all fours. All at once the place seemed to be alive with moving forms, and Heyward was about to give the crow call when a rustle of leaves drew his eyes in another direction.

About a hundred yards from him stood a strange Indian, also studying the low huts and the moving forms below. Heavy paint covered the fellow's face so that he looked more sad than savage. The hair of his head was cut except for the lock on the top, from which hung three or four hawk feathers. He wore a ragged cloth over a white man's shirt; on his feet were deerskin moc-

◇◇

casins. As Heyward looked curiously, the scout stole to his side.

"We have reached their village," whispered Heyward, "and here is another savage who makes things more difficult for us."

Hawkeye dropped his rifle into position and stretching his long neck, looked closely at the Indian.

"He is neither a Huron nor from the Canada tribes," he said. "But his clothes show that he has been stealing from the whites. Can you see where he has put his rifle or his bow?"

"He seems to have no weapons, and so, unless he spreads the alarm to his fellows down there in the water, we have little to fear from him," replied Heyward.

Hawkeye, looking at Heyward in surprise, opened his mouth wide in that silent laugh which danger had taught him to use.

"His fellows down there in the water!" he repeated. "So much for book learning! Keep your gun trained on him till I creep through the bushes and take him alive. Whatever happens, don't shoot!"

After several minutes, Heyward saw the scout creeping along the ground behind the Indian. Suddenly he heard several loud blows on the water, and a hundred dark forms disappeared. Then Hawkeye was upon the man with his hand lifted, but, instead of seizing him by the throat, he tapped him merrily on the shoulder.

"How now, my friend! Have you a mind to teach the beavers to sing?"

"The God who gave them power to do their work so well," came the ready answer, "would also give them voices to sing His praise."

CHAPTER 21

Heyward Takes
a Bold Chance

◇◇◇

ONE MAY imagine Heyward's surprise at finding that the "Indians" below were really animals, and the lake was a beaver pond. The "enemy" so near him was none other than David, the master of song. Finding him gave Heyward new hope, and, springing forward, he seized David's hand so eagerly in his own that he brought tears to the eyes of the good singer.

"You were about to start practicing song among the beavers, were you?" laughed Hawkeye. "Those clever fellows already know how to beat time with their tails, as you heard just now. I've known those who could read and write and still were greater fools than an old beaver. Now what do you think of a song like this?" Hawkeye gave the crow's call—the signal agreed upon—and soon the rest of the party appeared in answer. Hawkeye continued, laughing: "See! this music brings two guns to me, to say nothing of knives and tomahawks. But we see you are safe. Tell us what has become of the maidens."

"They are prisoners of the Indians," said David, "though safe in body."

"Both of them?" demanded Heyward.

"Both. We have had little to eat, but little to complain about except that we were led away against our wishes."

"Bless you for those words!" cried Munro. "Then I'll find my daughters!"

"I know not," replied David. "The leader of these savages is possessed by a devil that only the Lord can tame. I have tried him sleeping and waking, but neither words nor tunes seem to touch his soul."

"Where is he?" asked Hawkeye.

"He is hunting today with his young men. And tomorrow, I hear, they go farther into the forest and nearer to Canada."

"Where are the sisters now?" asked Heyward.

"The older maiden is with a tribe near by—the other

◇◇

side of that black rock. The younger is held among the Hurons. They live only two short miles from here."

"Then they are not together?" said Heyward. "Poor, gentle Alice!"

"So far as praise and the singing of psalms can quiet the spirit," returned David, "she has not suffered, but she weeps more than she smiles."

"And why are you left and not watched?" asked Heyward.

"Song has some power over even these heathen,[1] and I am allowed to go and come at will."

Hawkeye laughed and tapped his forehead, knowing that the Indians would not harm one of so simple a mind. Heyward made several wild suggestions for freeing the sisters. But Hawkeye pointed out to him that acting too quickly might only put the sisters in greater danger.

"Let this man go in again as usual," said Hawkeye, "and tell the maiden we are here. And, David, when you hear the call of the whippoorwill [2] three times, come to the call."

"I will go with him," said Heyward.

[1] *heathen,* person who does not believe in the God of the Bible.
[2] *whippoorwill,* a bird that calls at night. Its song sounds like its name.

"You!" cried Hawkeye. "Are you tired of seeing the sun rise and set?"

"The Hurons have shown mercy to David——"

"Yes," returned Hawkeye, "but David does some things that no man in his senses would do. They have no reason to fear him."

"I too can play the madman, the fool, the hero."—Heyward had a plan.—"I'll do anything to save the one I love, and I am determined to go!"

Hawkeye looked at him for a moment in complete surprise, for until now Heyward had followed the scout's directions in all matters.

"You know how to change me," he continued. "Paint me—change me to anything—a fool, if you wish!"

"Well," said Hawkeye, with little faith in this plan, "when I go to war, I like to be able to see who are my friends and who are my enemies, but——"

"Listen," said Heyward. "David tells us that the Indians are of two tribes. Cora, he thinks, is with the Delawares, Alice with the Hurons. While you are trying with your friends to free Cora, I'll try to free Alice."

Hawkeye saw danger ahead. Perhaps Heyward would take foolish risks to satisfy his love, but in the end the scout agreed to the plan.

◇◇◇

"Come on," he said with a smile. "The Great Serpent can find all kinds of colors here in the woods and he knows how to use them. Sit down on this log, and he will make a natural fool of you, and that to your liking."

The Mohican, knowing well the arts of the Indian, drew on Heyward's face lines that stood for fun and merrymaking. He was most careful to use none that stood for war. Because the Indians sometimes had players to amuse them, Heyward believed that he could pass for a wandering player from the French force at Fort Ticonderoga. Knowing how to speak French would help him.

When it was thought that he was painted enough to fool the Hurons, Hawkeye gave him advice and signals and named a place for meeting in case the parties should be successful. The parting from his friend Munro was a sad one. But Hawkeye promised to leave the old man in a safe place with the Great Serpent to look after him while the two search parties were away. The scout's last words to Heyward were:

"You have the hot blood and stout heart of the young man, but you will need a sharper wit than is learned from books if you beat the cunning and courage of a Mingo. God bless you! If the Hurons get your scalp, you have my promise that they will pay for it with a life for every hair it holds."

Heyward motioned to David to lead on. Their way lay across the clearing of the beavers, and around the lake until, as day was fading, they reached a place where they could see well into the opposite side of the clearing. Fifty or sixty rude huts had been built there and placed with no regard for order or beauty. Near by, twenty or thirty dark figures rose from the tall grass, then fell from sight like spirits. A thin, naked form was seen to toss its arms wildly in the air and disappear.

"These are children of the devil," said David. "Three nights have I been here, and three nights have I gathered these children for song, but their howlings freeze my soul."

Heyward's mind was not on David, but rather he looked about to get in mind a picture of the village.

"These young savages run wild," continued David. "In a country full of birches, no rod is ever used to correct a child, and so their time is wasted in such cries as you now hear," and he closed his ears to the young pack.

"Let us go on," said Heyward firmly.

CHAPTER 22

Running the Gauntlet

◇◇

THERE were no guards to warn the Indians of the coming of Heyward and David, and so they soon found themselves among the children at play. The children, however, raised a sharp, warning cry and then sank out of sight. This cry brought a dozen warriors to the door of the nearest hut, where they gravely waited.

David led the way into the largest hut in the village— one roughly made of bark and branches of trees—where the Hurons held their councils. As Heyward brushed past the strong, dark forms of the savages, his heart sank within him. He followed closely after David. Trying to appear brave, he walked to the center of the lodge, and there, again following David's example, seated himself on a pile of brush.

The warriors fell back from the door and formed a circle around him, waiting for him to speak. A low, smoking light was burning and throwing its red beams from face to face. Heyward tried to study these faces. The chiefs in front of him looked at him and then at the ground. Those in the shadows, he knew, were studying every line of his paint. This was an important moment for Heyward. Would they know that he was an enemy? If they discovered his plan, he would have to die a cruel death. At last one gray-haired man stepped up and spoke in the tongue of the Hurons.

"Do none of my brothers speak English or French?" asked Heyward in French. "I should be so sorry to think that no one of this wise and brave nation could understand the language which the Great Father, Montcalm, uses when he speaks to his children."

There was no answer. No one moved. At last the old Indian spoke.

"When the Great Father speaks to us, is it in the tongue of the Huron?"

Not knowing what this meant, Heyward played for time:

◇◇

"His children are all the same to him, whether they are red or black or white, but he likes the Hurons."

"How will he speak when our braves show him scalps that five nights ago grew on the heads of Yengeese?" [1]

"They were his enemies," said Heyward, shuddering. "Montcalm will say, 'It is good. My Hurons are very brave.'"

"His ears are open to the Delawares," said the Huron sadly, "and they are not our friends. They will fill him with lies."

"It cannot be. See, he sent me to his children, the red Hurons. I am to ask if any are sick, for I know the art of healing."

Every eye was again turned upon Heyward. The old man continued coldly:

"Do the wise men of the Canadas paint their skins? We have heard them boast that their faces are pale."

"When an Indian chief comes among his white fathers, he lays aside his own buffalo skins for the clothes they offer him. My brothers have given me paint, and so I wear it."

A low murmur told Heyward that the Hurons were

[1] *Yengeese*, Indian way of saying *English*. The word *Yankee* is thought to have come from this word.

pleased at this mark of respect, and he breathed more
freely. Next came a few minutes of silence, then a low
but terrible sound broke from the forest. This was followed by a high, piercing yell. With wild shouts, the
Indians rushed from the hut. Slipping out, Heyward
found himself in the center of a band of men, women,
and children, all clapping their hands and screaming in
mad pleasure.

A line of Indians came marching slowly from the
woods, the one in front carrying a pole from which hung,
as Heyward learned later, several scalps. The terrible
sound Heyward had heard was the death cry. Each time
it was heard, it told that another enemy had been killed.

The warriors stopped a few hundred feet from the
lodges. All were quiet for a moment. Then they called
out a signal, and in another moment all was hurry and
confusion. The warriors drew their knives, waved them
in the air, and then formed two lines from the war party

to the lodges. The women and even the children seized
knives or axes and took places in the lines, all eager for
the cruel game which was to come.

Within the clearing, around which grew tall, dark
pines, were piles of brush to which an old squaw now
set fire. In the glare of these fires, the mad scene was
frightful.

The returning warriors pushed forward two men who
seemed to have been chosen for the chief actors in the
game. One of them, a young man, stood straight and
firm as if prepared to meet any fate. The other was
bowed as if weighted down with shame. These two were
to run the gauntlet for their lives.

There was a signal for the two to run. The bowed man
did not move. The other sprang forward like a deer, and,
before a single blow could be struck, he leaped over the
heads of some children and darted toward the woods.
Some of the older men who stood farther back threw

themselves in front of him and drove him again between the lines. With the speed of an arrow he sprang through the flames of one of the burning piles of brush to the other side, trying to escape there. Here again he was met by the older Hurons and turned back. Time after time this happened. Arms and flashing knives waved in the air. The light form of the young man still escaped them, but human power could not long hold up under such a terrible strain.

In a last effort to reach the woods, the young man flew past Heyward. As a tall Huron pressed close after him with his knife lifted for the killing blow, Heyward put out his foot and the Huron fell. A moment later the young man, having gone the length of the line, was quietly leaning against a post by the door of the largest lodge. He was breathing thick and hard, but he gave no sign of suffering—and he was safe for the present. Since he had completed his run through the lines, the rules of the tribe would protect him at least until the council should decide his fate.

The Huron men were angry and sullen, for they had been tricked in their killing game. The women, with bitter laughs, spoke every curse they knew against him. To all this, the proud young man made no reply. Still

◇◇

more angry, the women screamed at him. The old woman who had lighted the fires pointed her finger at him and cried:

"Look you, Delaware, your nation is a race of women. The hoe fits your hand better than the gun. The Huron girls will make you short skirts and we will find you a husband."

The young man still made no reply. The old woman, more angry than ever, let forth a new flood of words. Others joined her. A young Huron waved his tomahawk in the captive's face. At that, he turned and Heyward looked into the eyes of none other than Uncas!

A Huron forced his way through the crowd, took Uncas by the arm, and led him into the council lodge, where the chiefs and the warriors took their places in the order of their rank in the nation. In the very center of their circle, under an opening that let in the light of two or three stars, they placed the quiet, proud Uncas. The other captive, who in shame had held back from the chase, was also led in. He was, as Heyward believed, a Huron warrior.

The old chief spoke to Uncas:

"Delaware, you are of a race of women, but you have proved yourself a man. I would give you food, but he who eats with a Huron should become the friend of the Huron. Rest in peace till the morning sun, when our last words shall be spoken."

"Seven days and seven nights I have fasted on the trail of the Hurons," Uncas replied coldly. "The Delaware children know how to travel the path of the just without stopping to eat."

"Two of our young men are after your companion," continued the chief. "When they return, then will our wise men say to you 'Live' or 'Die.' "

"Has a Huron no ears?" asked Uncas with scorn. "Twice has the Delaware heard a gun that he knows. Your young men will never come back!"

"If the Delawares are so wise, why is one of their bravest warriors here?"

"He followed a flying coward and fell into a trap." Uncas pointed at the captive Huron.

Now the old chiefs in the center talked together in short, broken sentences. Then followed a long silence. At last the oldest of the chiefs arose and addressed the second captive, who was still in his war paint, but whose every muscle trembled in his fear.

"Reed-that-bends," said the old man, "though the Great Spirit has made you pleasant to the eyes, it would be better that you had never been born. Your tongue is loud in the village, but in battle it is still. The enemy know the shape of your back, but they have never seen the color of your eyes. Three times have they called on you to come and as often you did not answer. Your name will never be heard again in the nation. It is already forgotten."

Shame and fear and pride showed in the face of the prisoner. He arose to his feet, bared his bosom, and looked at the shining knife that the judge held high. As the knife passed slowly into his heart, he fell heavily on his face at the feet of the straight form of Uncas.

The old squaw gave a yell, dashed the light to the earth, and buried everything in darkness. The Hurons shuddered and slipped out of the hut like troubled spirits.

CHAPTER 23

Uncas Is Sentenced to Death

◇◇

THE MOMENT the Hurons were gone, a strong hand was laid on Heyward's arm and Uncas whispered in his ear:

"Hurons are dogs who will soon know that the sight of a coward's blood can never make a warrior tremble. The Gray-Head [1] and my father are safe, and Hawkeye's rifle is not asleep. Go! Uncas and the Open Hand [2] no longer know each other. It is enough."

Heyward wanted to know more, but at a gentle push from Uncas he started toward the door. It must not be known now that he and Uncas were friends. Out in the

[1] *Gray-Head*, Colonel Munro.
[2] *Open Hand*, Major Heyward.

open the dying fires threw a dim light on the figures that stole about the village. A ray of light through the open door showed Uncas still standing, and the dark forms of the Hurons carrying the dead man out.

Heyward walked about among the lodges in search of some news of Alice. Finding nothing, he returned to the council lodge, walked in, and seated himself. The warriors were again smoking and talking over the Horicon affair. Uncas remained where Heyward had left him. The only sign that he was being watched was an armed warrior in the doorway. Heyward did not wish to talk, but one of the older Hurons spoke to him in French:

"My Canada father does not forget his children. I thank him. An evil spirit lives in the wife of one of my men. Can the wise man drive it away?"

Heyward knew something of the practices of the Indian medicine men; he also thought it might be a good chance to learn news. But he must continue to act in his new character, and so he answered with quiet dignity:

"Spirits not all alike. Some give up to power of wise man. Some, too strong."

"My brother is great medicine," said the anxious man. "He will try?"

◇◇◇

Heyward nodded. Satisfied, the Huron took up his pipe and waited the proper time to move. It seemed an hour before he laid aside the pipe and was about to go to the sick woman. Just then, another Indian of large, strong body walked in and sat down near Heyward, whose flesh began to creep, for it was Sly Fox. Several pipes were now lighted, and the room was filled with smoke before anyone spoke.

"Welcome!" said one. "Has my brother found the moose?"

"The young men bend under their loads," replied the Fox.

Then another chief spoke:

"The Delawares, like bears after honey, have been around this village. But who has ever found a Huron asleep?"

"The Delawares of the lakes?" cried the Fox in a voice like thunder.

"No! those who wear the skirts of women. One of them has been near the village."

"Did my young men take his scalp?"

"His legs are good, though his arm is better for the hoe than the tomahawk," returned the other, pointing to Uncas.

◇◇◇

The Fox shook the ashes from his pipe, placed his tomahawk in his belt, arose and looked for the first time at Uncas. Uncas turned suddenly to the light and they met face to face. The eyes of Uncas opened like those of a lion at bay.[3] The Fox's look changed to one of cruel joy. Then in a loud voice he spoke the name "Bounding Elk!"

At the sound of this name, every warrior sprang to his feet. That hated and yet respected name was repeated as if by one voice. The women outside the door repeated it. The eyes of all turned toward the young Mohican who had so often proved his skill against the proudest of the Hurons. The Fox, raising his arm, shook it at Uncas so that the silver ornaments on it rattled.

"Mohican, you die!" he shouted.

"The Huron men are squaws," said Uncas with scorn. "Their women are owls. Go! Call the Huron dogs that they may look upon a warrior. The Mohican is not pleased. He smells here the blood of a man afraid!"

This insult sank deep within the Hurons. Dropping the light robe of skin from his shoulders, the Fox stretched out his arm and burst out with words of hate. His fame

---

[3] *bay.* Here the word means the stand taken by a hunted animal when it is cornered and cannot escape.

as a speaker always brought him many listeners and now he spoke with more force than ever, for he thirsted for revenge. He told of the attack at Glenn's, the death of his fellows, and the escape from their enemy. He told of their later capture, and how his plan to kill the maidens was broken by the party of the Long Rifle. Then he lowered his voice to speak of the Huron dead.

"Are the bones of my young men in the burying place of the Hurons? No. Their spirits are gone toward the setting sun, to the happy hunting grounds.[4] But they

[4] *happy hunting ground.* The Indians' idea of heaven was a place for wonderful hunting.

◇◇◇

left without food, without guns or knives. Shall this be? Shall their souls go hungry? What will our fathers think of the Hurons? Brothers, we must not forget the dead. A red man always remembers. We will load the back of this young Mohican with food and guns till he falls and send him after our young men. When they see him toiling after them, they will go on happy. A stain on the name of a Huron can be hid only by blood from the heart of an Indian. Let this Delaware die!"

The Fox had so played on the feelings of these men that one ugly old warrior arose and, giving out the yell of a devil, threw his ax at Uncas. The Fox shot out his hand and caught it. Uncas stood still, eying his enemy with cold scorn. The Fox spoke again:

"The sun must shine on his shame. The squaws must see him tremble. Take him away."

Uncas was bound and led out. At the door he turned and eyed his enemies proudly, and Heyward felt that not all hope was gone. The warriors again took up the pipe and passing it from one to the other, filled the place with their smoke. When the chief who had asked for Heyward's help had finished, he motioned with his finger for the "medicine man" [5] to follow. Heyward was

---

[5] *medicine man*, Indian doctor.

glad at last to breathe the pure air of a cool summer evening.

Instead of going to the lodges where Heyward still hoped to find Alice, the chief turned aside toward the foot of a mountain that towered high over the village. They passed up a narrow winding path and through another clearing. Here the children had returned to their play and, trying to make their game like the awful one they had just seen, had set fire to other piles of brush. These fires lighted the way for Heyward and the chief. As they crossed the clearing, the light fell on a strange, huge creature in their path. What at first looked like a great black ball began to move with a slow, rolling step. Then a growl told that it was a bear.

The Huron went on and Heyward went with him, thinking that this was one of the tame bears sometimes found around Indian camps. But Heyward was uneasy and looked back often. The bear still followed. Heyward would have spoken, but at this moment the Indian pushed back a door of bark and entered a cave in the mountain.

Heyward was about to close the door when he felt it pulled from his hand by the beast, which followed him inside. Now they passed through a long, narrow open-

ing in the rocks. Heyward pressed on, keeping as close
as possible to the Huron. The bear growled at his heels,
and once or twice its huge paw was laid on him as if to
hold him back. Heyward's fears were growing when he
saw a light ahead.

In a large cave they found the sick woman, whom the
Indians believed to be in the power of evil spirits. Beside her bed were some squaws and, to Heyward's surprise, his missing friend, David.

One look told Heyward that the sick woman was beyond human help, but, to gain time, he still prepared to
carry out his plan. David, on the other hand, wanted to
try the power of music. From his pitch pipe he took his
key and began to sing a hymn. As the song continued,
Heyward was shocked by a sound half animal, half human. Looking around, he saw that it came from the
bear, which was sitting up, swinging its big body from
side to side in time with the music and giving out its
low, strange growls.

The effect on David can be better imagined than
told. He doubted both his eyes and his ears. His voice
caught in his throat. He ended his song quickly with
"She expects you and is near at hand," and then he
dashed out of the cave.

CHAPTER 24

The Bear That Sang Like a Man

◇◇◇

IN THE dim shadows the bear continued to swing from side to side while Heyward looked from it to the sick woman and back again. David's parting words troubled Heyward. What had David meant?

The chief walked to the bed of the sick woman and motioned the others away. Although they were curious to see the skill of the new medicine man, they obeyed. A moment later the door of the outer cave closed.

"Now let my brother show his power," said the chief.

Heyward knew that to wait would be dangerous. He prepared at once to try a form of magic of which he had heard, and might have given himself away had he not been stopped by a fierce growl from the bear. Three

❖❖

times he tried and each time that fierce growl stopped him.

"The spirits want to be alone," said the Huron. "I go. The woman is the wife of one of my braves. Be just to her." Then, turning to the bear, he said "Peace!" and left the cave.

The bear seemed to listen till the door had closed; then he lumbered up to Heyward and sat up like a man. His whole body shook. He pawed at his head. Suddenly the bear's head fell to one side and in its place appeared the honest face of Hawkeye.

"Be quiet!" he said quickly. "These varlets are all around the place, and any sound but that of a medicine man would bring them back in a body."

"Tell me the meaning of this," gasped Heyward when he could speak. "Why have you tried such a dangerous trick?"

"Have you seen Uncas?" asked Hawkeye.

"To my great sorrow, yes. He is a prisoner of the Hurons and is to die at the rising of the sun."

"That is my real reason for being here," said Hawkeye. "I could never leave the boy to the Hurons. They would have a glorious time if they could tie the Bounding Elk and the Long Rifle to the same stake."

"But how did you get here?" asked Heyward.

"Well, Uncas and I came upon a returning party of Hurons. The lad was too bold, but, being of hot blood, he wasn't much to blame. Then one of the Hurons proved a coward and, in running away, led Uncas into a trap."

"That Indian paid for it with his life and his honor," said Heyward.

"The man who is afraid doesn't live long with the Indians," said Hawkeye. "Then when I saw that I was alone, I followed here. Luck led me to a lodge where I found one of their witch doctors [1] with this bearskin, getting ready to battle an evil spirit. A rap over the head quieted him, and I made off with this skin—and here I am."

"You make a good bear, too," laughed Heyward.

"I've studied them in the woods, and I know the nature of the beast. But there is work to be done. Where is the gentle one?"

"I have looked in every lodge in the village," said Heyward sadly.

"You heard the singer say, 'She expects you and is near at hand.' I'll have a look around."

[1] *witch doctor*, another term for "medicine man."

◇◇

Hawkeye climbed to where he could see over the wall.

"She is here," he whispered back. "But in that paint you might make her lose her reason. Wash your face in that spring that runs out of the rock."

When he had washed the paint from his face, Heyward disappeared through the passage and found Alice —pale, weak, and anxious, but still lovely.

"Duncan," she cried with the greatest joy, "I knew you would come to me!"

Heyward told her quickly how he and Hawkeye had come for her and, as she listened, hardly breathing, new hope came to her.

"I can't take time now to express my wishes," said Heyward, "but your father is safe, and he understands my love for you."

As Heyward bent over to lift her in his arms, he felt a light tap on his shoulder. Turning, he found himself face to face with Sly Fox. A deep laugh sounded in the throat of the savage. Heyward's first thought was to throw himself on the Fox and fight it out, but he had no weapons and for the sake of Alice felt that he must play safe.

With fire in his eye, he watched his enemy. The Fox drew back and pushed a log across the opening of the room. Then, having made sure of his prisoners, he spoke:

"The palefaces trap the cunning beavers, but the red men know how to take the Yengeese."

"Huron, do your worst!" exclaimed Heyward, forgetting for the moment to keep cool. "I despise you and your spirit of hate!"

"Will the white man speak those words at the stake?" asked the Fox.

"He will speak them to your face or to your whole nation!"

"The Sly Fox is a great chief," returned the Indian. "He will bring his young men to see how bravely a paleface can laugh at death."

As he turned to leave, a growl caught his ear and there in the door was the bear, rolling from side to side. The Fox saw that this was only the witch hunter (as he thought) and would have passed it by. But the bear reared up on its hind legs and threw its front legs around the Indian, pinning his arms at his sides with a powerful bear hug. Heyward caught up a cord of deerskin and rushed upon the Fox, tying him tightly. His arms and legs were tied round with many folds of the deerskin.

◇◇◇

Hawkeye pushed a gag into the mouth of the Fox, and the Huron was laid on the floor.

Now Hawkeye took the bearskin from his head and showed his face to the Fox with a merry laugh. Then he turned to Heyward.

"Bring the gentle one," he said. "We must make a push for the woods."

"She is too weak to walk," said Heyward.

"Wrap her in them Indian clothes. Cover that little foot. There is no other like it in all these woods. Now carry her and leave the rest to me."

Heyward eagerly took the light form of Alice in his arms and set out behind the scout. Outside the entrance to the cave a murmur of voices told them that the friends of the sick woman were there waiting for news of her.

"If I speak," whispered Hawkeye, "they will know that I am a white man. Give them your medicine talk, Major. Say that we have shut the evil spirit in the cave and are taking the woman to the woods to find roots to make her strong."

The scout opened the door and, still wearing the bearskin, lumbered past the crowd. Heyward kept close at his heels and soon found himself in the center of a group of about twenty people. The crowd fell back to let the husband and the father speak.

"Has my brother driven away the evil spirit?" demanded the father. "What has he in his arms?"

"The evil spirit is gone out of her," replied Heyward. "It is shut in the rocks. I take her away to find roots to make her strong again."

"I will enter the rock and fight the evil one," said the father.

"Is my brother mad?" cried Heyward in alarm. "He will meet the disease and it will enter him. Or he will drive it out and it will chase the daughter into the woods. Let my children wait outside and, if the spirit comes, beat it down with clubs."

The father and the husband both obeyed. Instead of entering the cave, they drew their tomahawks and waited. The women and children broke branches from trees or seized rocks to fight the spirit, but Heyward and Hawkeye disappeared.

Hawkeye knew the Indians' fear of spirits. He knew, too, that if he aroused the least doubt on the part of the Indians, all might be lost. He hurried Heyward away,

◇◇

keeping to the outside of the village. Alice, feeling better now in the open air, was able to walk. When they
were some distance from the lodges, Hawkeye stopped.

"This path will lead you to a brook," he said. "Follow the north bank till you come to a fall. From the hill
to the right you will see the fires of the other Indian
people. Go to them and ask them to help you. If they
are true Delawares, you will be safe. Go, and God help
you."

"But you!" cried Heyward. "Surely we are not to
part here?"

"The Hurons hold Uncas—the last of the high blood
of the Mohicans," replied Hawkeye. "I must see what
can be done. If the young man is led to the stake, I shall
fight the Hurons till I die. You have risked your life
to save this gentle one, but, as for me, I taught Uncas
to use the rifle, and well has he paid me for it. In many
a bloody fight, so long as I could hear the crack of his
gun and that of his father, I knew that no enemy was
at my back. Winters and summers, nights and days we
have wandered through the woods together, eaten together—one sleeping while the other watched. And it
shall not be said that Uncas was taken to the cruel

stake while I was at hand. As long as my Killdeer shoots true, the Mohican boy shall not die for want of a friend."

With that, the scout turned back to the lodges and Heyward and Alice turned toward the distant village of the Delawares.

CHAPTER 25

Tricks of the Medicine Man

◇◇◇

HAWKEYE now set out to save Uncas, and yet he knew full well the dangers that were ahead. His enemies were watching as closely as he. They did not trust strangers, and they never forgot an injury. He would feel much safer now if he had killed the Huron witch doctor, and the Fox. An Indian would not have hesitated to kill them, but such an act would not be worthy of a white man.

As he neared the village, he watched for signs that might help him. A half-finished hut stood some distance from the others, with a dim light shining through its cracks. He decided to see what was there. With his bear suit on, he crawled toward the opening and looked in. There was David, the faithful singer. He was dressed as before except that on his head he wore a three-sided, cocked hat.[1] He was sitting on a pile of brush feeding some pieces of wood into the fire, his head leaning on his arm, his face wearing a most puzzled and frightened expression. He believed in the miracles [2] of which the Bible told him, but he had never expected a miracle in his own life. Now he himself had just heard a bear sing. What could it mean?

Before speaking to David, Hawkeye made a circle around the hut to see if they were alone. Then he walked through the low door. David looked at him from the other side of the fire, too frightened at first to speak. Then he searched for his pitch pipe, hoping that music might quiet the beast.

"Dark monster!" he cried, "I know not what you want with me, but listen to the words of the young man of the Bible and spare me!"

The bear shook his shaggy sides and a well-known voice said, "Put up that tooting thing. Five words of plain English will be worth more just now than all of your singing."

"What are you?" demanded the poor singer.

[1] *cocked hat*, a hat used at that time. It was turned up on three sides to form three points.

[2] *miracle*, a wonderful happening—one not in keeping with the laws of nature.

◇◇◇

"A man like yourself, with no blood of bear or Indian —no more than yourself."

"Can such things be?" David was breathing more freely now. "I have seen many wonders among the Indians but nothing to equal this."

"Come, come," returned Hawkeye, putting his head out through the opening in the skin. "Now let us get down to business."

"Where are the maiden and the young man?" asked David.

"They are free from the tomahawks of these varlets. But can you tell me anything about Uncas?"

"The young man is here and I am afraid he is to die," said David sadly, "and I have found a hymn——"

"Can you lead me to him?"

"Yes, but your presence will not help his unhappy state," continued David.

"No more words, but lead on," demanded Hawkeye, putting his face again under the skin.

The lodge in which Uncas was held was in the very center of the village, where it was hard to go in or out without being seen. But Hawkeye, in his bearskin, boldly took a straight path to the place. The late hour made it easier, for most of the people of the village were now sound asleep. Only four or five of the warriors were hanging around the door.

When David came toward them with what they thought was one of their witch doctors, the warriors made way for both. As the scout did not know the Huron language, he had to trust David to do the talking. Although he was a simple fellow, David played his part well.

Speaking to the savages, he said: "The Yengeese, my white brothers, have told the Delawares to take up the tomahawk and strike their fathers in the Canadas. But the Delawares are women. Does my brother wish to hear the Bounding Elk ask for his skirts, and see him weep before the Hurons, at the stake?"

Replies of "Hugh" told what a pleasure this would be to the Hurons—how much they would enjoy this show of weakness on the part of Uncas.

"The cunning man will blow upon the Delaware dog," said David. "But, my brothers, stand back or his breath might take away your courage, too."

The Hurons quickly fell back. The scout entered the place and came near to Uncas, who was half sitting, half lying in a dark corner. Bound by strong and painful bands, the young Mohican paid no attention to the

◇◇

animal, which he believed to have been brought in to test his courage. After lumbering about with his slow, rolling walk, the scout changed his growl to a low hiss.

Uncas turned at once and whispered, "Hawkeye!"

"Cut the bands!" ordered Hawkeye.

David did so and Uncas found himself free. Hawkeye, keeping himself in the shadows, slipped out of the bear-skin and handed his knife to Uncas, saying: "The Hurons are outside. Let us be ready."

"Let us go to the Turtles," [3] said Uncas. "They are the children of my grandfathers."

"Yes, Uncas, the same blood runs in your veins, I believe. But what shall we do with the Mingoes at the door? There are six of them and the singer is as good as nothing."

"The Hurons boast," said Uncas with scorn. "They run like snails, while the Delawares run faster than deer."

"Your legs are strong enough, but the gift of a white man lies more in his arms than in his legs," said Hawkeye. "I can brain a Huron, but they might prove too much for me in a race."

---

[3] *Turtles*, the Delawares, and especially that branch of Delawares to which Uncas belonged.

Uncas had drawn near to the door, but, seeing that Hawkeye hesitated, he returned.

"Uncas will stay," he said simply. "He will fight with his brother and die with the friend of the Delawares."

"Ah, Uncas," said Hawkeye, pressing the boy's hand, "it would have been more like a Mingo than a Mohican if you had left me. Put on this skin. You can play the bear as well as I."

Uncas put on the skin, as he had been told to do. Then Hawkeye spoke to David. He hoped with David's help to carry out a daring plan by which both of them might escape.

"Friend," he said, "you will be more comfortable in my clothes than in the ones you now wear. Take my hunting shirt and cap. Give me your blanket and hat. Give me your book and spectacles and tooter, too. If we ever meet again in better times, you shall have them all back, and with many thanks.—Are you afraid?"

"My acts are those of peace and love," replied David, as each put on the other's clothing, "and I trust the Lord even in the greatest danger."

"Your greatest danger will be when the Indians find that they have lost Bounding Elk," said Hawkeye.

◇◇

"Take the place of Uncas and make them believe we forced you to do it."

"Uncas has battled for me," said David firmly. "I will dare as much for him."

"Said like a man!" replied Hawkeye. "Hold your head down and keep quiet as long as you can. When you do speak, break out in one of your songs. I believe you are safe, but if they take your scalp Uncas and I will have revenge."

"Hold!" exclaimed David. "I am not one who believes in revenge. Should I fall, kill no one, but forgive them and pray for their good."

The scout thought this over.

"That is not the law of the woods," he said. "But it is noble, and I do believe you are right. God bless you, friend."

So saying, the scout shook David's hand and joined Uncas, who was now the bear. Waving his arm as David did to keep time, he began a song. When they reached the door, one of the Hurons put out his arm to stop the singer.

"The Delaware dog!" he exclaimed. "Is he afraid? Will the Hurons hear him groan?"

A fierce growl came from the beast, so natural that the Huron jumped aside. Hawkeye did not dare speak, for his voice would have given him away. He again burst out in song and the Indians willingly let him and the witch doctor, as they thought, pass by.

Time was now needed to make sure of their safety, for their attempt was bold and open, and the hour was dark. Soon they got clear of the village and found the shelter of the woods. The Mohican had no more than time to throw off his bearskin when a long and loud cry rose from the central lodge. In a moment a burst of cries filled the air and ran through the whole village. The scout picked two rifles from where they had been hidden under a bush. One he handed to Uncas, then waving Killdeer over his head, he exclaimed:

"Now let the devils hunt us. We'll take at least two scalps before we die."

Then they dashed forward and were soon buried in the darkness of the forest.

◆◇◆◇◆◇◆◇◆◇◆◇◆◇◆◇◆◇◆◇◆◇◆◇◆◇◆◇◆◇◆◇◆◇◆

PART FIVE

War between the Hurons and the Delawares

CHAPTER 26

Hawkeye Rescues Uncas

✧✧✧

THE INDIANS who had stood around the prison of Uncas had feared the breath of the witch doctor, but at last they dared to peep through an opening of the hut. They saw David and for a few minutes believed that he was Uncas. But David became tired and stretched out his long legs till his big feet could be plainly seen in the light of the fire. Not knowing that he was being watched, he turned his head and they saw his face. Then they rushed into the hut, laying their hands on him, and saw how they had been tricked. At once the cry arose that Uncas and Hawkeye had heard from the forest. The Hurons burst out with angry yells and cries for revenge.

◇◇◇

David, who was firm in his wish to help his friends, thought his hour had come. He had neither his book nor his pipe, but his memory still served him, and he broke out in a loud song. Remembering his weak mind, the Indians did not harm him. Instead, they rushed out to awaken the village.

The sounds of alarm brought out two hundred men, ready for battle or for a chase. Hearing of the escape, the whole tribe crowded into the council lodge, eager for orders from their chiefs. And the chiefs were glad that Sly Fox was in the camp with his cunning and his wisdom. But where was the Fox? When his name was called, all looked around in wonder, and messengers were sent to his lodge, only to find it empty.

While some were searching for him, other swift men were ordered to make a circle of the village to see that their neighbors, the Delawares, were making no attack. Women and children ran about, and, in fact, the whole camp seemed to have gone wild. But soon the oldest and wisest of the chiefs met.

Shouts from many voices told that a party was coming and might throw some light on these strange affairs. The crowd before the door fell back and several braves entered, bringing with them the unhappy witch doctor whom Hawkeye had hit on the head when he took over the bearskin. Some of the Indians did not believe in the power of this man, but all listened to his story with sharp interest. Then the father of the sick woman stepped up to tell what he knew.

Here, surely, was a many-sided puzzle. Ten of the wisest chiefs were chosen to solve it. They went first to the cave where the sick woman lay. They found her lying just as they had left her although the father and many others said they had seen her carried away by "the medicine of the white man." The puzzle grew deeper than ever. When it was found that she was dead, her father hid his face in sorrow. Then, pointing to his daughter, he said:

"She has left us! The Great Spirit is angry with his children."

The silence that followed was broken only when a dark object rolled out of the next room into the very center of the group. All drew back in the greatest surprise, but when the object rolled into the dim light they were even more surprised to see the fiercely angry face of Sly Fox. Several knives were whipped out and the

◇◇◇

Fox's limbs and tongue were set free. The Huron stood up and shook himself like a lion in his cage. He spoke not a word but seized the handle of his knife while his eyes searched the group as if seeking an object for revenge.

Had Uncas or Heyward or Hawkeye been present then, he would surely have been severely punished. Sly Fox snapped his teeth together like jaws of steel, but, seeing only his friends about him, he swallowed his anger. One of the oldest of the party spoke:

"Sly Fox has found an enemy. Is he near, that the Hurons may take revenge?"

"Let the Delaware die!" roared the Fox.

"The Mohican is swift of foot and leaps far," said the old chief, "but my young men are after him."

"Is he gone?" cried the Fox.

"An evil spirit is among us and the Delaware has blinded our eyes."

"The same evil spirit," sneered the Fox, "that has taken the lives of so many Hurons, the spirit that has killed my men at the Tumbling River, that took the scalps at the Healing Spring, and that bound the arms of Sly Fox."

"Who, my friend?"

"The dog with the heart and cunning of a Huron under a white skin—The Long Rifle."

The sound of that terrible name had the usual effect on the Hurons. When they learned that he had been in their very camp, black rage took the place of wonder. They bared their teeth; they beat the air as if their enemy were there before them. Then the Fox changed his manner. He would make the Hurons believe that he knew perfectly how to find and capture Heyward, Hawkeye, and Uncas.

"Let us go to my people," he said. "They wait for us."

They went back to the council lodge, where all eyes were turned on the Fox. With his excellent gift of speech, he told all that had happened to him: how cunningly Heyward and Hawkeye had tricked him—how they had also tricked the tribe. When he had ended and taken his seat, the fighting men looked at each other, wondering at the success of their enemies' daring plan as well as at the boldness of the insult. Now, how could they get revenge?

More young men were sent to find the trail of Hawkeye and Uncas, while the chiefs talked together. The

◇◇◇

Sly Fox listened, and, now that he was again in command of himself, he quietly laid his own plans. Before long some of the young braves returned to say that the trail of the enemies lay in the direction of the Delawares. This was all the Fox needed to know to complete his scheme.

He had kept Alice here among his own people, the Hurons. Cora, whom he valued more than her fair-haired sister, he had sent to his neighbors, the Delawares. In putting Cora in their care, he felt that he was flattering the Delawares. More than that, he had Alice entirely in his power.

Several of the chiefs suggested quick ways of surprising the Delawares, taking their camp, and getting the prisoners, for all agreed that honor demanded the death of those who had tricked them.

The Fox was able to point out that each of the plans suggested would be too difficult to carry out. And now he was ready to offer his own plan—a plan which was slower but more sure and, more important to Sly Fox, one which would put him in a position of power among the Hurons.

He began by flattering the braves. He spoke of their

courage and their wisdom. Wisdom, he told them, marked the difference between the beaver and the other animals, between the animals and man, between the Hurons and the rest of men. In their wisdom they must move against their enemies slowly and carefully, but in the end they would enjoy a complete victory and again have control of their old hunting grounds and their own villages.

So well did he flatter that the Hurons agreed to his plan, and Sly Fox was chosen to direct the whole affair. It was a happy moment for the Fox—now he was the ruler of the Hurons; he could rule with an iron hand.

Spies were sent to look into the camp of the Delawares. The braves were sent back to their own lodges, to meet Sly Fox in the morning. The Fox returned to his hut where he lived alone, for the wife he had left when he was chased from the Hurons was dead and he had no children. He did not try to sleep—instead he spent the night thinking over the wrongs which he fancied had been done to him and his thirst for revenge.

Long before day broke, twenty braves came to him. Each carried his rifle although the paint on each face was the paint of peace. When all were ready, Sly Fox

gave the order to march. In single file they followed
their leader and slipped from the camp like spirits.

CHAPTER 27

In the Camp
of the Delawares

◇◇◇

THE DELAWARES whose camp was so near had about as many warriors as did the Hurons. Like the Hurons, they had followed the French into the lands of the English, but they had not chosen to help Montcalm in his attack on Fort William Henry. Instead, they had sent him word that "their hatchets were dull and would have to be sharpened," and as Montcalm did not want to make enemies of them, he said nothing further.

On the morning when Sly Fox led his silent party from the camp of the Hurons, the Delaware camp was a very busy one. The women ran from one lodge to another, some preparing the morning meal, some whispering to each other. The warriors gathered in groups,

◇◇◇

but few were speaking. Some of the braves were examining their guns with unusual interest. All eyes turned at times toward the large lodge in the center of the village, as if it contained the thing of which they were all thinking.

Suddenly a man appeared on a high, flat rock at the edge of the village. He carried no arms. He stopped in full view of the Delawares to make a sign of peace by throwing his arm up toward heaven, then letting it fall on his breast. Being answered by the same sign from the village, he walked in among the Delawares. The only sound as he came on was the rattling of the light silver ornaments on his arms and neck, and the tinkle of the little bells on his moccasins.

When he reached the group of the principal chiefs he stopped, and only then did the Delawares see that he was the well-known Huron chief—Sly Fox.

"The wise Huron is welcome," said a Delaware chief. "He is come to eat with his brothers of the lakes."

"He is come," said the Fox, with a dignity worthy of a prince.

Each chief held out his arm and, taking each other by the wrist, they gave the Indian's friendly greeting. These two then went with several of the old men to the

Delaware's lodge, where they talked for a time about the hunting trip of Sly Fox. All knew that some secret object was in the Fox's mind, but all pretended to think the visit a thing of little importance. Then there began a battle of wits.

"Is the face of the great Canada father turned again toward his Huron children?" asked the Delaware chief, Hard Heart.

"When was it not so?" returned the Fox. "He calls my people 'most loved.'"

The Delaware, knowing how troubled Montcalm had been because of the massacre, continued:

"The tomahawks of your young men have been very red."

"But they are now bright and dull, for the Yengeese are dead and it is the Delawares who are now our neighbors."

A wave of Hard Heart's hand answered this flattery. Then, speaking of Cora, the Fox asked:

"Does my prisoner give my brother trouble?"

"She is welcome."

"If she troubles my brother, let her be sent to my squaws," said the Fox.

"She is welcome," repeated Hard Heart, and the Fox

❖❖

began to wonder if the Delawares meant ever to give Cora back to him.

"Do my young men leave the Delawares room on the mountains for their hunting?" he continued.

"The Delawares rule their own hills," replied Hard Heart coldly.

"That is well," said the Fox. After a pause he asked, "Have there not been strange moccasins in the woods? Have not my brothers seen the marks of white men?"

The Delaware did not answer this directly.

"Let my Canada father come," he said. "His children are ready for him."

"The Canada father is welcome among the Hurons, too," replied Sly Fox. "But the Yengeese have long arms. They have legs that never tire.—My young men dreamed that they had seen the marks of the Yengeese near the village of the Delawares!"

"The Delawares will not be found asleep."

What did this mean? Sly Fox wondered, but he answered:

"I have gifts for my brother."

He arose and spread his gifts before the eager eyes of the Delawares. They were gifts of little value—things that had been taken from the dead bodies at Fort William Henry, but the Delawares were pleased. Their chief spoke again:

"My brother is a wise chief. He is welcome."

"The Hurons love their friends, the Delawares," returned Sly Fox. "Why should they not? Their skins have the same color." Then he added: "Has not my brother seen spies in the woods?"

The gifts had loosened the tongue of Hard Heart and he answered:

"There have been strange moccasins around my camp. They have been tracked into my village."

"Did my brother beat the dogs?" asked Sly Fox.

"It would not do. The stranger is welcome with the Delawares."

"The stranger, but not the spy," said Sly Fox. "The Yengeese have sent out their scouts. They have been in my camp, but they found no welcome there. Then they came to the Delawares, for they call the Delawares their friends. The Canada father will think the Delaware hearts are turned away from him."

This thrust had the effect which Sly Fox had wanted. The Delawares had not helped the French in their attack on Fort William Henry. But still they wanted to be considered friends of Montcalm because their villages, their hunting grounds, and many of their women and children were in land now held by the French. These English people who had come to them were enemies of the French, and so they must be treated as enemies of the Delawares.

"Let my father look in my face," said Hard Heart in some alarm. "He will see no change. My young men had dreams because they did not go on the warpath, but they love the great white chief."

"Will he think so when he hears that his greatest enemy is fed in the camp of his children?—When he is told that the Yengee who has killed so many of his friends is with the Delawares and smokes at their fires? Canada father is not a fool!"

"Where is this Yengee? Who is it that has taken the lives of my young men? Who is the enemy of my great father?" demanded Hard Heart.

"The Long Rifle!"

The Delawares started now at hearing this name, showing by their surprise that they had not known such a famous man was in their village.

"What does my brother mean?" asked Hard Heart.

"A Huron never lies!" replied Sly Fox. "Let the Delawares look at their prisoners and see."

◇◇

There was a short council of the chiefs of the tribe.
Then a meeting was called of the whole nation. Within
a half hour all were present—every man, woman, and
child. They numbered about a thousand.

In a meeting as serious as this, no young brave would
ever be so bold as to speak. First, rather, the oldest and
wisest man in the nation would lay the subject of the
meeting before the people. Until he spoke, no one else
would dare to move. On this occasion the oldest chief
in the tribe was silent for a long time, but at last he
arose.

His body, which had once been tall and straight like
the pine, was bent under the weight of more than a
hundred years. His face was dark, with deep lines mark-
ing it. His dress was rich but simple. His robe was of the
finest skins and covered with picture writing. The front
was hung with rich pieces of silver, and the handle of his
knife shone like solid gold.

Now from mouth to mouth was whispered the name
of Tamenund. Sly Fox had often heard of this wise and
just Delaware, who it was said had been blessed with
the rare gift of talking in person with the Great Spirit.
The Huron stepped out a little from the crowd to get a
better view of the noble old man. He saw that the old

◇◇

man's eyes were closed as if he had grown weary of man's troubles.

Again there was a complete silence which told of the deep respect in which this old chief was held by his people. Directions were whispered to some of the young braves, who left the lodge and returned in a few minutes bringing the prisoners before the court. The crowd opened a path through which the prisoners passed, then closed in a circle around them.

CHAPTER 28

A Strange Shooting Match

◇◇◇

IN SPITE of the savage faces on every side, Cora seemed anxious only for her trembling sister, Alice. Close beside them stood Heyward, and Hawkeye brought up the rear. Uncas was not there. After the usual long, quiet wait, one of the chiefs asked in good English:

"Which is The Long Rifle?"

At first neither Heyward nor Hawkeye spoke. Heyward's eyes looked around the dark, silent crowd and saw the hated Sly Fox. He knew it was this cunning savage who was plotting to kill him and his friends, and determined to stop him. He had seen an Indian punished. He feared that Hawkeye might be punished in

◇◇

the same way, and he would protect his friend if it was at all possible. The question was repeated.

"Give us arms," said Heyward, "and let them answer."

"You are the Long Rifle, whose name has filled our ears!" cried the chief. "What has brought the white man into the camp of the Delawares?"

"I come for food, shelter, and friends."

"That cannot be. The woods are full of game. A warrior needs no shelter but the sky. The Delawares are enemies, not friends, of the Yengeese."

Hawkeye stepped forward.

"I am the Long Rifle," he said. "I am not afraid to tell you, neither am I ashamed."

All eyes turned from Heyward to Hawkeye and back again. Which was really the Long Rifle? To be so great a scout was an honor any man might be glad to claim, but the Delawares wanted to be just and there must be no mistake. Some of the old men talked together and decided to ask Sly Fox. The Huron pointed to Hawkeye.

"Will a wise Delaware believe the barking of a wolf?" exclaimed Heyward. "A dog never lies, but when was a wolf ever known to speak the truth?"

The eyes of Sly Fox flashed fire, but he turned away,

knowing that he must remain calm and that the Indians would soon get the truth. The Delaware continued:

"My brother has been called one who lies, and his friends are angry. Let the prisoners speak the truth with guns."

Guns were placed in the hands of the two friends, and they were ordered to fire at a small bowl lying on a stump about fifty yards away. Heyward smiled at the thought of his trying to beat Hawkeye, but he would try and perhaps he might learn more about the plot of Sly Fox.

Raising his rifle with great care and aiming three times, he fired. The bullet cut the wood a few inches from the bowl—a good shot, as the Indians knew. Even Hawkeye nodded his head. A young Indian touched him on the shoulder and asked:

"Can the paleface beat that?"

"Yes!" cried Hawkeye, raising the gun in his right hand and shaking it at Sly Fox. "Yes, Huron, and I could strike you now if I should choose to send a bullet through your heart. No power on earth could stop me. Why should I not? Why!—because I might bring down evil on innocent heads. If you know such a being as God, thank Him that you are still alive!"

◇◇

All held their breath, not knowing what might happen, till an old chief said, "If the white man is a great warrior, let him strike nearer the mark."

The scout laughed aloud; then, dropping the gun easily into his left hand, he seemed to shake it. The gun fired and pieces of the bowl flew into the air. A murmur from the crowd showed their admiration for this great skill. But many seemed to think the success was pure accident. Heyward helped them toward this opinion.

"It was chance!" he cried. "No one can shoot that well without aim."

"Chance!" cried Hawkeye. He might lose his life because of his excellent shooting, but he was still proud of it. "Does that lying Huron think, too, that it was chance? Give him another gun and put us face to face, and we'll decide that matter."

The old Delaware spoke again:

"The hawk that comes from the clouds can return when he wishes. Give them the guns."

Hawkeye seized a gun while Sly Fox watched him with growing fear, but the scout turned to Heyward.

"Now let us see which is the better man," he cried. "You see that gourd hanging against the tree, Major? Let me see if you can hit it."

The gourd hung by a cord of deerskin from a tree about a hundred yards away. Heyward, too, knew that his life was at stake, but he felt a great desire to win this match. He aimed with the greatest care and fired. The ball hit the tree right beside the gourd. The warriors held their breath and turned to Hawkeye.

"That may do for the Royal Americans," said Hawkeye, laughing, "but if my aim missed that much, many a bloody Mingo would still be alive." He raised his rifle

◇◇

and stood still as a stone for a moment—then a sheet
of flame burst out. A young Indian ran forward but
could find no trace of the bullet.

"Go!" said the old chief with scorn. "You are a wolf
in the skin of a dog. I will talk to Long Rifle of the
Yengeese."

"Fools!" stormed Hawkeye. "If you want to find the
bullet, look *in* the gourd!"

One of the Indian boys tore the gourd from the tree.
With a shout, he pointed to a hole in it. A cry of admiration broke from the crowd, and now indeed they knew
which really was the Long Rifle. The old chief turned
to Sly Fox: "Brother, the Delawares listen."

This was just the chance Sly Fox wanted. He stood
up and walked slowly and proudly to the center of the
circle. He looked at the earnest faces before him. He
looked at the prisoners, and at last spoke:

"The Spirit that made men made them of different
colors. Some He made with pale faces, and these He
ordered to be traders and dogs to their women. He made
them wish for the whole earth. He gave them tongues
like the wildcat with the cunning of the hog, but not
with the cunning of the fox. With his tongue the pale-

face tells lies to the Indians. He pays warriors to fight his battles. By his lies he gets the goods of the earth. The Great Spirit gave him enough but he wants all. Such are the palefaces.

"Some the Great Spirit made with skins as red as the sun, and these He made like Himself. He gave them this land covered with trees and filled with game. The sun and rain ripened their fruits, and the snows came to make them thankful. If they fought, it was to prove that they were men. They were brave, and just, and happy."

He looked around. All eyes and ears were turned toward him. He went on:

"Some of His people He placed among the snows, some near the setting sun, some on the land around the great fresh waters. But to his greatest and most loved He gave the sands of the salt lake. Do my brothers know the name of the most loved people?"

"It is the Delawares!" cried twenty eager voices.

"That is true," said Sly Fox with his head bowed. "The sun rose in water that was salt and set in water that was sweet, but always it smiled on the Delawares. But why should I, a Huron of the woods, tell a wise peo-

◇◇

ple their own story? There is no one among them that has not seen it all and does not know that it is true. I have done. My tongue is still, for my heart is heavy. I listen."

All the while Hawkeye was proving his skill at shooting, and while Sly Fox was speaking, Tamenund had remained quiet. Now all eyes were turned toward him. Slowly he raised himself to his feet.

"Who is this that calls upon the Delawares?" he asked. "Who speaks of things gone? It is better to thank the Great Spirit for that which remains."

Sly Fox stepped near to the high place where Tamenund stood.

"It is a friend of Tamenund—a Huron."

"Is the Huron our friend?" asked Tamenund. "What brings a Huron here?"

"Justice," replied Sly Fox. "His prisoners are here and he comes for his own."

Tamenund turned his head, asking another chief to explain; then, facing Sly Fox, he said:

"Justice is the law of the Great Spirit. Huron, take what is yours and go!"

The old man seated himself and closed his eyes as if

better pleased with his own memories than with the things now happening.

Several young braves stepped up at once and bound Heyward and Hawkeye with strings of deerskin. Sly Fox motioned them to follow him. Then, knowing that Cora would follow wherever Alice might be taken, he picked the young girl up in his arms and started out from the circle. But Cora threw herself at the feet of Tamenund and cried:

"Just and wise Delaware, give us mercy! Do not listen to this beast who poisons your ear with lies that he may satisfy his thirst for blood. You have lived long and learned many things. You will know how to help those who suffer."

The eyes of the old man opened heavily. Slowly he turned and saw her on her knees before him.

"Who are you?" he asked.

"A woman," replied Cora. "A Yengee—but one who has never harmed you or your people. One who asks for your help."

"Many summers have come and gone," said the old man, "since I drank from the waters of my own rivers. The children of the white men were greedy. They came

◇◇

and took our rivers and our lands for themselves. Do they follow us even here?"

"We follow no one," replied Cora, "and all we ask is to go in peace. Are you not Tamenund, the father, the judge—yes, the prophet [1] of his people?—Seven years ago one of your people was at the mercy of a white chief. He was of the blood of the good and just Tamenund. 'Go,' said the white man. 'For Tamenund's sake, you are free.' Do you not remember?"

But Tamenund had forgotten. Cora struggled to make him understand.

"Tell me," she asked. "Is Tamenund a father?"

"He is the father of a nation."

"Oh, father who is just! I ask nothing for myself, but there,"—she pointed to Alice—" is the daughter of an old man whose days are near their close." Then she pointed to the Sly Fox. "She is too good for anyone so wicked."

But the old man's mind was wandering. If only she could make him understand!

"There is another prisoner here," she said, "one of your own color. Let him speak!"

[1] *prophet*, person who tells what will happen.

"It is a snake," said another Delaware. "It is a red man in the pay of the Yengeese. We have kept him to burn at the stake."

"Let him come," said the old man and he sank back again to his seat while all waited without a word.

CHAPTER 29

Sly Fox Calls Upon the Ancient Law

◇◇

THE DELAWARES waited until the circle had opened and shut again, and Uncas stood in the center. All eyes were on the young Mohican as he looked around at the faces of his enemies. When he saw Tamenund, all else was forgotten. With noiseless step he took his place before the aged chief, where he stood, straight and proud.

"With what tongue does the prisoner speak?" asked Tamenund.

"Like his fathers," answered Uncas, "with the tongue of the Delaware."

Angry voices answered this, and the old man passed his hand before his eyes as if to wipe away a shameful sight. Then he spoke again:

◇◇

"A Delaware! I have seen the tribes of the Delawares driven from their council fires and scattered among the hills of the Iroquois! I have seen the beasts of the mountains and the birds of the air come to live in the wigwams of men. But never before have I found a Delaware so low as to creep like a snake into the camps of his own nation."

"The singing birds [1] have returned," said Uncas softly, "and Tamenund has heard their music."

The old father started and turned his head as if to catch a passing song.

"Does Tamenund dream!" he exclaimed. "What voice is in his ear?"

He seemed lost in thought and his people waited, for it might be that he was again speaking directly with the Great Spirit. At last one of his chiefs called his mind back to the prisoner.

"The false Delaware trembles in fear of the words of Tamenund. He is a dog that howls when the Yengeese show him a trail."

"And you," returned Uncas, "are dogs that sit up when the Frenchman throws you the waste parts of the deer!"

[1] *singing bird*, a liar.

◇◇◇

Twenty knives flashed in the air and twenty braves jumped to their feet, but one of the chiefs quieted them.

"Delaware, little worthy of the name!" said Tamenund. "The warrior who leaves his tribe when his people are in trouble is twice bad, and the Great Spirit is just. My children, the prisoner is yours. Deal justly by him."

An angry cry broke from the circle, and savage yells told how eagerly they would take the prisoner to the stake. Heyward struggled madly with those who held him, and the eyes of Hawkeye looked about anxiously. Again Cora threw herself at the feet of the old man, begging for mercy.

Uncas alone remained calm. He looked on his enemies with a steady eye, and when they came to seize him he faced them firmly. One among them, if possible more fierce than the others, seized the hunting shirt of the young Mohican and tore it from his body. In a moment his eyes started, his mouth fell open, and his whole frame seemed frozen in complete surprise. His companions crowded around in wonder, and every eye fastened itself on the figure of a small turtle beautifully tattooed in bright blue on his breast.

Uncas smiled and, motioning the crowd away, he

stepped to the front of the nation with the air of a king
and called out:

"Men of the Delawares! My race holds up the earth!
Your weak tribe stands on my shell. What fire could
your braves light that would burn the child of the Turtle? The blood of my fathers would smother the flames!
My race is the grandfather of all nations!"

"Who is this?" demanded Tamenund.

"Uncas, the son of Great Serpent," answered the
young man, bowing his head before the gray-haired one.
"I am the son of the Great Turtle."

"The hour of Tamenund is near!" exclaimed the old
chief. "I thank the Great Spirit that one is here to fill
my place at the council fire. Uncas is found. Let the eyes
of a dying eagle look on the rising sun!"

The young man stepped lightly forward. Tamenund
held him at arm's length and read the lines in his face.
Then he spoke:

"Does Tamenund dream? His arm is weak now like
the branch of a dead oak, yet Uncas is before him as
when they went into battle against the palefaces! Uncas,
the lion of his tribe, the son of the Turtle, the wisest of
the Mohicans! Tell me, Delawares, has Tamenund been
asleep for a hundred winters?"

◇◇◇

Only Uncas dared to answer. "The blood of the Turtle has been in many chiefs," he said, "but all have gone back into the earth except the Great Serpent and his son."

"It is true! It is true!" returned the father of the tribe, as the memory of it came back to him. "Our wise men have often said that two of our warriors were in the hills of the Yengeese. Why have their seats at the council fires been so long empty?"

Uncas raised his voice so all could hear:

"Once we slept where we could hear the salt lake speak. Then we were rulers and chiefs over the land. But when a paleface was seen on every brook, we followed the deer back to the river of our nation. The Delawares were gone. Then said my fathers, 'Here will we hunt. Toward the setting sun we would find streams that run into the great lakes of sweet water, but there would the Mohican die like fishes of the sea in a clear spring. When the Great Spirit is ready and calls us, we will follow the river back to the sea, and take our own again.' Delawares, this is what the children of the Turtle believe. Our eyes are on the rising sun, not on the setting sun, and we shall go back."

Uncas watched the effect of his words, and he was

◇◇

satisfied. He stepped over to Hawkeye and, with a quick stroke of his knife, cut the cords that bound him. He led Hawkeye by the hand to the feet of the old chief.

"Father," he said, "this paleface is a just man, and a friend of the Delawares."

"What name has he gained by his deeds?" asked Tamenund.

"We call him Hawkeye, for his sight is always true. The Mingoes know him better by the death he gives their warriors. They call him the Long Rifle."

"The Long Rifle!" exclaimed Tamenund, sternly. "My son has not done well to call him friend."

"He has proved himself a friend," returned the young chief. "If Uncas is welcome among the Delawares, then is Hawkeye with friends."

"The paleface has killed my young men."

"The Mingo who whispers that is a singing bird!" said the scout. "I have killed the Mingoes, even at their own council fires, but I have never knowingly hurt a Delaware."

"Where is the Huron?" asked the old man.

Sly Fox had seen the Delawares nodding, for they knew that Hawkeye had spoken the truth. He had seen

◇◇◇

the victory of Uncas. But he would still try to get his prisoners.

"The just Tamenund will not keep what a Huron has left in his charge?" he asked.

The old chief continued to speak to Uncas:

"Tell me, my son, has the Huron a conqueror's right over you?"

"He has none," replied Uncas. "The mountain lion may get into traps, but he is strong and knows how to leap through them."

"The Long Rifle? Has the Huron a right over him?"

"He laughs at the Mingoes," said Uncas.

"The stranger and the white maiden that came into my camp together? What of them?"—Tamenund was trying to be just.

"They, too, should journey on an open path," Uncas told him.

"And the woman the Huron left with my warriors?"

Uncas made no reply.

"She is mine!" cried Sly Fox in triumph. "Mohican, you know she is mine."

"My son does not speak," said the old chief, hearing nothing from Uncas but seeing the sorrow on his face.

"It is so," was the low answer.

At last the wise one, knowing the law of the Indian, said sternly:

"Huron, go!"

"Must the Huron go as he came?" asked the cruel Fox. "The wigwam of Sly Fox is empty."

Speaking to Cora, the old chief asked, "Girl, what would you have? A great chief would take you to wife, and your race would never end."

"Better a thousand times that it should!" cried Cora.

But Tamenund pronounced his sentence:

"Go, Huron. Take thine own. The Great Spirit tells the Delaware to be just."

The Huron seized Cora. The Delawares fell back, but Heyward ran forward.

"Huron, have mercy!" he cried. "And you shall have gold that will make you richer than any of your people have ever been."

"Sly Fox wants not the toys of the palefaces."

"Gold, silver, powder, lead—everything a warrior needs," added Heyward.

"The Fox is strong enough, and now he has his revenge."

Heyward turned then to Tamenund. "Mighty ruler, Tamenund," he cried, "I beg you for mercy."

"The words of the Delaware are said," replied the old man.

Hawkeye turned to the Fox. "Huron," he said, "many a Mingo has fallen before my rifle and I'll meet many more Mingoes in the woods. Instead of the maiden, would you take me—unarmed?"

"Will the Long Rifle give his life for the woman?" demanded the Fox.

"I have not said as much as that," answered Hawkeye. "But I might go to your camp for six weeks, if you will let the maiden go."

As the Fox shook his head, the scout added: "I would give you my gun and teach your young men to shoot."

When the Fox only grunted and started through the circle, Hawkeye spoke to his friends:

"The varlet knows his power. I'll go in the maiden's place. It's likely they would get my scalp sometime anyway, and a day or two sooner won't make much difference. God bless you, Uncas," he said with a catch in his voice. "I loved you and your father and, as honest men, we'll meet again in the next world. You will find the rifle where I hid it." Then he turned to Sly Fox.

"Huron, I am your prisoner. Let the woman go."

Even the fiercest of the Delaware warriors showed their admiration for such a manly sacrifice. The Fox hesitated a moment. Then, noting again Cora's beauty, he motioned with his hand and answered:

"Sly Fox is a great chief. He does not change his mind. He will go." He put his hand on Cora's shoulder and pushed her ahead of him.

"Noble scout," said Cora to Hawkeye, "with all my heart I thank you. I could not accept your offer and let

◇◇

you go to your death, but will you do this?—See that my sister is given back to Father?" Then, turning to Heyward, she said:

"Duncan, you love her. Take care of her. God bless you all," and she turned to go with the Huron.

Fired with anger, Heyward shouted: "Go, Huron! By the laws of these Delawares, they cannot stop you, but I have no such law, and I can follow."

With a cruel smile the Huron answered, "The Open Hand can come."

Uncas, still not willing to give up, broke in:

"Huron, your path is open and short. Soon the sun will be seen above the trees. Then there will be men on your trail."

"I hear a crow!" said Sly Fox with scorn. "Go!" he added, pushing Cora. "Where are the skirts of the Delawares? Let them send their arrows and guns to the Hurons, and then hoe corn. Dogs! Rabbits! Thieves!— I spit on you!"

And Sly Fox and his prisoner passed into the forest. The Fox had won his battle.

CHAPTER 30

Uncas Prepares for Battle

THE MOMENT Sly Fox and Cora disappeared into the forest, the crowd seemed filled with fierce anger. From a high rock, Uncas had kept his eyes on Cora till the colors of her dress were lost in the green of the woods. Then he came down, and, as he moved through the crowd, the Delawares caught the flash of anger in his eyes. He walked into the lodge from which he had been led only a short time before.

From that same lodge a young brave soon came forth in a very serious march toward a small pine that grew out of a rocky cliff. He tore the bark from the body of the tree and returned to the lodge. Soon a second came and cut the branches from the tree, leaving only the

◇◇

bare trunk. A third painted the tree with stripes of dark-red paint. Outside, the other men neither spoke nor moved as they watched these preparations for battle. Last, the young Mohican himself came out, stripped of all clothing except his girdle and leggings, and painted with the signs of war.

With slow steps he moved toward the post and began to march around it—still with a slow, measured step, at the same time raising his voice in a wild war song. The notes were sad at first, rising then till they trembled with power. The words were a kind of hymn to the Great Spirit—a prayer for His help.

Put into English, the words would be about like this:

"Great Spirit! Great Spirit! Great Spirit!
Thou art strong, thou art good, thou art wise.
Great Spirit! Great Spirit!
Thou art just.

"In the heavens, in the clouds, oh, I see
Many spots—many dark, many red.
In the heavens, oh, I see
Many clouds.

"In the woods, in the air, oh, I hear
The whoop, the long yell, and the cry.
In the woods, oh, I hear
The loud whoop!

"Great Spirit! Great Spirit! Great Spirit!
I am weak—thou art strong. I am slow.
Great Spirit! Great Spirit!
Give me help!"

After the third verse, the terrible war cry burst from the lips of the young chief. Then in the last verse, as in the first, he begged for help. Three times he sang the song and three times he circled the post with his dance.

Then followed a chief of the Delawares, singing words of his own to the same sad, wild tune. Warrior after warrior now joined in the dance, as it grew wilder and wilder. They twisted their bodies, whirled their tomahawks, made fierce faces. Uncas, stepping forward, struck his tomahawk deep into the post and raised his voice in a loud shout, a war whoop of his own. By this act he announced that he himself would lead in the coming fight.

Now a hundred young men rushed to the post—their fancied enemy—and chopped the "enemy" to pieces until nothing remained but the roots in the earth. This fierce delight spread till the war became a war of the whole nation.

The moment Uncas struck the blow, he moved out of the circle and looked at the sun. It had almost reached the top of the pine; now no law would protect Sly Fox. A call from Uncas stopped this mock war and started preparations for the real one.

The face of the whole camp changed quickly. The warriors, already armed and painted, were still. The women went about the village with songs in which joy and sorrow were strangely mixed. Tamenund had a last touching meeting with Uncas, whom he looked upon as a child once lost but now brought home. Heyward, having helped Alice to a place of safety, looked for Hawkeye.

Since the scout had heard this war song many times he paid little attention to it, but looked about over the warriors, glad to see how many had answered Uncas' call to battle. Knowing that Sly Fox would have spies in the woods, Hawkeye dared not go out himself to the place where he had hidden Killdeer and the gun of Uncas when they had come into the Delaware camp. But a boy could go there, for the Hurons would not fear him. Hawkeye chose a boy he thought smart enough for the errand and told him just what he wanted done.

Almost bursting with pride at the trust placed in him, the boy walked carelessly out of the village and entered the woods. There he threw himself on the ground and crept like a serpent toward the treasure. He found it and a moment later he came flying back across the clearing, bearing a prize in each hand. He was leaping up the sides of the rough rocks when a shot rang out. The boy answered it with a shout. Another bullet was sent after

him, but he reached the village and, holding the guns up
in triumph, carried them to Hawkeye. After looking the
pieces over carefully and snapping the hammers a dozen
times, Hawkeye turned to the boy, asking in his kind
way if he was hurt. The boy looked up proudly but
made no answer.

"Ah, I see, lad, the Mingoes have barked your arm,"
said Hawkeye, taking the arm, which did indeed have a
deep flesh wound. "But a little crushed alder [1] will act
like a charm, and I'll wrap it in a band of wampum. You
are a warrior early, my brave boy. Many young men
have taken scalps and cannot yet show a mark like this.
In time you will be a chief."

The boy, true to his Indian training, was more proud
of that flowing blood than he would have been of a gold
prize. With his head high, he walked among the other
boys of his age, admired and envied by all.

Although the boy won little praise at the time from
the busy chiefs, his brave act served to show the Delawares that Huron spies were near and a party was sent
to drive them out. This was soon done, for the Hurons,
seeing that they had been discovered, began to draw
back. Uncas called his forces together and divided du-

---

[1] *alder*, a small tree. The Indians believed its sap would help heal wounds.

ties among them. Scouts were sent on ahead. In Hawkeye's charge he placed twenty men. He would have placed as many under Heyward, but Heyward asked only to help the scout. The duties of each chief were laid before him, and word was given to move forward. More than two hundred men obeyed.

As they crept into the forest, they found nothing to cause alarm. Nor was there anything to give them any information until they came upon their own scouts. Here the chiefs were called together for a whispered council. Had Uncas followed his own wishes, he would have attacked at once. But such a plan would not have been in keeping with the practices of the Delawares, and so he forced himself to a slower plan.

During this meeting of the chiefs a man was seen coming alone from the side of the enemy. He came on quickly, making some think him a messenger of peace. But when he stopped, seeming puzzled as to which way to go, all eyes turned to Uncas.

"Hawkeye," said the young chief, "he must never go back to the Hurons."

Hawkeye raised his gun, but, instead of firing, he burst into his quiet laugh.

"I took him for a Mingo," laughed Hawkeye. "But

when my eye ran along his ribs for a place to put the
bullet in—what do you think, Uncas?—they were a
white man's ribs and not an Indian's." Then Hawkeye
crept through the brush to bring David in safely.

"Now tell us about the Mingoes," said Hawkeye
when he and David had joined the others. "And do it
without any ups and downs of voice."

David looked at the circle of Indians. Then, getting
control of himself, he replied:

"The Hurons are out in large numbers and with evil
in their hearts. They have been howling like wolves and
talking such language that I came to the Delawares for
peace."

"Where are they?" asked Hawkeye.

"Hid in the forest between here and their village, and
in such force that if you are wise you will return at
once."

Uncas asked about Sly Fox.

"He is among them. The maiden he brought from the
Delawares, he took to the cave. Like a wild wolf, he is
at the head of his savages. I know not what has troubled
his spirit so greatly."

"It's well we know where the cave is," said Heyward.
"Let us go at once."

"What says Hawkeye?" asked Uncas.

"Give me twenty men. I will turn to the right along the stream and pass the huts of the beavers. There I will join your father and Colonel Munro. When you hear the war cry from that quarter, Uncas, drive in their front. We'll carry their village and take the woman from the cave. We'll do it, as you Indians say, by dodge and cover.[2] There may be no great learning in this plan, Major, but with men brave enough it can be done."

"I like your plan," cried Heyward. "Let us go quickly."

After a short council, orders were given to the different parties and again they moved forward.

[2] *by dodge and cover*, by jumping quickly from one hiding place to another.

CHAPTER 31

Revenge Is Bitter

◇◇◇

BETWEEN the Delawares and the village of their enemies all was quiet, but Hawkeye knew the Hurons too well to trust appearances. He threw his gun into the hollow of his arm and led his group into the bed of the creek.

"Men," he said, "we'll keep under the cover of the banks of this stream till we scent the Hurons."

At this point his men pointed to David, who had followed after them. Hawkeye tried to tell the poor singer how serious and how dangerous was the work ahead of them, but David firmly replied:

"Though not a man of war, yet gladly would I strike a blow for the maiden whom you seek, whatever may be the cost."

"Remember," said Hawkeye, "we have come to fight and not to sing songs."

David nodded and, since he could not be left alone in the woods, he was allowed to follow.

For about a mile their way led along the bed of the stream. To guard against a surprise attack, two Delawares crept on ahead, one on each side of the stream, watching at every move for possible enemies. Every few minutes the band stopped to listen, and Hawkeye was all eyes.

"We shall have a good day for a fight," he said to Heyward. "Both the sun and the wind are in our favor. But here is the end of our cover, for the beavers in their hundred years here haven't left many trees standing."

The stream sometimes shot through narrow openings between the rocks, and at other times spread out over wide stretches of low land, forming ponds. Hawkeye examined closely the dead trees, the moss, and everything about the place. He knew that the Huron camp was only a half mile up the stream, and he was troubled at finding no sign of the enemy. Once or twice he felt like ordering a rush on the village. But he decided this would not be wise and gave the order, instead, to go on slowly. As his party stole up the bank, a dozen rifles

◇◇◇

were heard behind them, and a Delaware, leaping high into the air like a wounded deer, fell dead.

"I feared something like this!" exclaimed Hawkeye. "To cover, and charge!"

The Hurons fell back and Hawkeye set his men an example of pressing after them. He ran from tree to tree as his enemy slowly drew back. But as the Hurons were joined by others of their tribe, their fire became nearly if not quite as heavy as that of the Delawares. Hawkeye's band was in great danger. When it seemed that the enemy was surrounding him, he heard shouts and the sound of arms from the trees where Uncas was posted below.

This fire from Uncas turned the Hurons at once. They had left too small a force to hold off the young Mohican, and so the battle rolled now from the forest toward the village. Many of the Hurons drew back to protect their homes. Hawkeye gave the order to bear down on them. From cover to cover the Delawares pushed nearer and nearer to the enemy. For a moment Heyward and Hawkeye found themselves behind the same tree.

"Shall we charge now?" asked the Major.

"I don't hunger for a rush just now," said Hawkeye. "A scalp or two would be lost—and yet, if we are to be of any use to Uncas, we must get rid of these varlets in front of us."

Then he called aloud to his Indians and motioned to them. The answer was a shout. Each warrior made a swift move from his own tree, then quickly dodged behind another. So many dark bodies in front of the Hurons drew a swift fire. Then the Delawares, knowing that the enemy guns were empty, leaped toward them, like so many wildcats springing upon their prey. Hawkeye was in front swinging old Killdeer and cheering on his men. A few of the more cunning Hurons, however, had not been deceived into shooting, and now fire from their guns felled three of Hawkeye's men. But the Delawares could not be stopped; they swept away everyone they met.

For a few moments, the two forces fought hand to hand. The Hurons drew back rapidly till they reached the opposite edge of the brush, where they hung on to the cover like hunted beasts. When the success of the fight seemed most in doubt, a bullet came whistling from among the beaver huts, followed by a fierce cry.

"That's Great Serpent!" shouted Hawkeye to his fellows. "Now we'll catch these Hurons in face and in back!"

◇◇◇

The Hurons, being attacked now from all sides, had no cover. They broke off and spread themselves across the opening, so that many fell under the bullets of the Delawares.

There was a short meeting now between Great Serpent and Hawkeye, and between Munro and Heyward. Hawkeye pointed out Great Serpent to his men and turned over his command to the Mohican chief, who led the men back into the brush. They went on then to a high bit of ground where there were trees enough for cover. From there the land fell away in front, and below them were several miles of deep, narrow woods. In this heavy forest Uncas was still fighting the main body of the Hurons. Great Serpent and his friends went to the brow of the hill and listened to the sounds of the fight.

"The fight is coming up the hill," said Heyward, pointing in the direction of the new firing. "We are too near the center to help much."

"They will follow the hollow where the cover is thickest," said Hawkeye, "and that will leave us well on this side of them. Great Serpent, lead on your men. We'll stay here and not a Huron shall cross behind you without a word from Killdeer."

The chief listened to the battle sounds and knew that

at this point the Delawares were winning. Hawkeye and his three friends stepped back a few steps to a shelter and waited. Before long the reports of the rifles told that the fight was again in the clearing. Here and there warriors appeared at the edge of the forest, gathering at the clearing as if to make a final stand. Others joined till many figures were seen hiding in the cover at the edge of the forest. Heyward looked anxiously toward the Great Serpent, who was sitting on a rock very calmly waiting.

"The time has come for the Delawares to strike!" said Heyward.

"No, not yet," replied Hawkeye. "See, the varlets are getting in those pines like bees. By the Lord, even a squaw might put a bullet into the center of such a bunch of dark skins!"

At this point Great Serpent gave a whoop and a dozen Hurons fell. A single shout answered, and then a cry went up as from a thousand throats. The enemy fell away from the center of their own line, and Uncas, at the head of a hundred warriors, rushed from the forest into the clearing.

Waving his arms right and left, the young chief pointed toward the enemy. The Hurons, now divided into two wings, were hotly pressed back into the woods, but one little group refused to seek cover. Like cornered lions, they backed up the hill that Great Serpent had just left. In this party Uncas saw Sly Fox, fighting fiercely.

Too eager to catch the Fox, Uncas dashed ahead till he found himself nearly alone. His cry of battle brought six or seven braves to his side, and, not thinking how he was outnumbered, he rushed upon the enemy, while the Fox watched with secret joy. But the Long Rifle, seeing the danger that faced his young friend, gave a great shout and, with his white helpers, rushed to the rescue. The Hurons turned at once and began running up the cliff.

Uncas swept after the Fox with the speed of the wind. Hawkeye called to him to take cover, but the young man, braving the fire of the Hurons, soon forced them to flee. If Hawkeye and his party had not been near to help, Uncas probably would have fallen because of his own lack of care. Hurons and Delawares entered the village within striking distance of each other.

The enemy made a stand at their council lodge, fighting desperately. The tomahawk of Uncas, the blows of Hawkeye, and even the nervous arm of Munro were so busy that the bodies of their enemies were soon scattered over the ground. The Sly Fox was daring, but still he escaped every effort against his life.

Some of the Delawares stopped to take the scalps of the dead, but Uncas leaped on after the Fox with Hawkeye, Heyward, and David close after him. The Fox leaped into the brush, reached the cave, and entered it. Now Hawkeye felt they were sure of their game.

The Hurons ran through the dim passages of the cave with Uncas and the others close after them. Then as the light grew more dim, they thought they had lost the chase. But Uncas caught sight of a white robe disappearing through a dark passage that seemed to lead up the mountain.

"It's Cora!" cried Heyward.

This sight of the girl gave them new courage, but the way was rough and broken, and in spots very difficult. So eager was Uncas that he threw away his rifle and sprang forward without arms. Then a gun at the end of the passage roared out, giving the Mohican a slight wound on the shoulder. Still he went on.

"We must close!" cried the scout. "They will pick us off at this distance, and they are using the maiden to shield themselves."

◇◇◇

Uncas got near enough to see that Cora was being hurried away by two braves, while Sly Fox urged them on. Then the forms of all four were seen clearly for a moment as they dashed from the cave through an opening in the mountain. Uncas and Heyward ran out of the cave in time to see that the way taken by the Hurons lay up a difficult and dangerous mountain path. But, weighted down with Cora, the Hurons were losing ground.

"Stop, Huron dog!" cried Uncas, shaking his tomahawk at the Fox.

The Hurons had come to a level bit of rock over a steep cliff near the top of the mountain. Suddenly Cora stopped.

"I will go no farther!" she cried. "Kill me if you will, but I will go no farther!"

The two Hurons raised their tomahawks with savage joy, but the Fox held them off and drew his own knife.

"Woman, choose!" he cried. "The wigwam or the knife of Sly Fox!"

Cora dropped to her knees, seeming not to hear. She raised her eyes and arms to heaven, and said quietly, "Lord, I am Thine. Do with me as You will."

The Huron trembled, raised his arm, then dropped it.

◇◇

At that moment a piercing cry was heard from a rock farther up the mountain and Uncas appeared, leaping upon them from that great height. As the Fox jumped back, one of his own men plunged his knife into the breast of Cora.

The Fox sprang like a lion on the murderer, but the falling form of Uncas came between them. Maddened by the loss of his most prized prisoner, the Fox buried his knife in the back of Uncas as he fell on the ground. Uncas, with his last bit of strength, raised himself. Like a wounded wildcat, he struck the murderer of Cora to his death. Then he turned to the Fox with a steady look that told plainly what he would have done if he had had the strength. The Fox fell upon the helpless Delaware and plunged his knife three times into the breast of the brave young chief.

"Huron, you will die for this!" cried Heyward from above.

Throwing his bloody knife up at Heyward, the Fox gave a cry so fierce, yet so joyous that it carried with it all the sounds of savage triumph. He was answered by a cry from Hawkeye, who moved boldly toward him among the sharp rocks. The Fox leaped a wide gap where another spring would have carried him out of

reach. There he stopped to look back at Hawkeye, shake his fist, and shout in scorn:

"The palefaces are dogs! The Delawares are women! Sly Fox leaves them on the rocks to the crows!"

Laughing wildly, he made a strong leap, fell short, but with his hand grasped a tree on the edge of the height. Hawkeye stood like a beast about to spring. His body trembled so that the half-raised rifle shook like a leaf in the wind. The Fox let his body drop to the length of his arms and found a rock for his feet to rest on. But Hawkeye trained the never-failing Killdeer on him, and fired. The body of the Fox fell back a little as he turned a cruel look upon his enemy and shook a hand in hate. But his hold loosened, his dark form glided past the pines that clung to the mountain, and Sly Fox dropped to an awful death on the rocks far below.

CHAPTER 32

The Victors Mourn

◇◇◇

THE RISING sun found the Delawares a nation of mourners. Although they had won their battle against the Hurons and had destroyed the whole Huron group, no shouts of joy or songs of triumph were heard. These would not have been in keeping with the deep sorrow of the Delawares and their white friends. Yet there were songs—soft, sad ones—as the Indian maidens sang the death songs of the tribe. And David was there with his little book of hymns and his pitch pipe. And the songs he sang were in keeping with the sad spirit that hung over the village of the Delawares that day after the battle.

And there was weeping. The Indians wept over the loss of their heroes, and Munro over his daughter, and the Great Serpent over his son Uncas—the last of the Mohicans. All in the village were sad. For the lives that had been given up were closely related to the whole tribe. And the dead were laid away to rest with the love and respect so well deserved by each.

Tamenund, the feeble old chief, was crushed, for he had felt that in Uncas he had found one worthy to carry on his high office. Tamenund, whose wisdom had for a hundred years been the spirit of the Delawares, was helped to his feet to speak to his people.

"Men of the Delawares! The face of the Great Spirit is behind a cloud! His eye is turned from you! His ears are shut! His tongue gives no answer! You see Him not, and yet His judgments are before you! Let your hearts be open and your spirits tell no lie. Delawares, the face of the Great Spirit is behind a cloud!" So he spoke his sorrow at the great loss he and his people suffered.

Great Serpent, with a heavy heart, stood with Hawkeye by the grave where Uncas lay buried. And from his years he spoke, not so much to the crowd as to himself:

"Why do my daughters and my brothers weep? Because a young man has gone to the happy hunting grounds? Because a chief has filled his time with honor?

He was good. He was brave. The Great Spirit has need of such a warrior, and has called him away. And I, the son and the father of Uncas, am left a stripped pine in a clearing of palefaces. My race has gone from the shores of the salt lake and the hills of the Delawares. But who can say that the serpent of his tribe has forgotten his wisdom? I am alone!"

"No, Great Serpent, not alone," said Hawkeye, who was deeply touched by the sadness of his friend. "Our skins are not the same color, but God has placed us here to journey together down the same path. Like you, I have no family and no people. He was your son, and by blood he was nearer to you, but I shall never forget him. The boy has left us for a time, but, Great Serpent, you are not alone."

Great Serpent grasped the hand of the scout. Two strong men of the woods, they stood with bowed heads and tear-filled eyes, looking at the ground that now covered one who for so many years had been a part of their very lives.

There was nothing now to hold the white visitors in the camp of the Delawares. Heyward pressed the hand of the scout and called to mind that they had agreed to meet again within the posts of the British army. And

Heyward felt bound by another tie, by another promise. For he loved Alice, and each was deeply thankful that the other was saved. Now that Cora was gone and Munro had grown so weak, Alice needed Heyward's love and care.

The young Indians had made a stretcher on which to carry the weak and tired Alice down from the mountains and into the settlements. Horses were brought for Heyward and Munro. David was to follow on foot, and Hawkeye would see them well on their way. A guard of a half-dozen strong Indians stood ready to go down the dark trail to help and protect the party.

Great Serpent and Tamenund, the two most powerful warriors of a day that was passing, stood together as Tamenund lifted his voice so that all his people might hear:

"It is enough. Go, my children of the Delawares. The anger of the Great Spirit is not done. Why should Tamenund stay? The palefaces are masters of the earth, and the time of the red man has not come again. My day has been too long. In the morning I saw the sons of the Turtle happy and strong. And yet, before the night has come, have I lived to see the last warrior of a wise race—the last of the Mohicans."

About This Book

In *The Last of the Mohicans*, we have a type of story dear to the heart of every American boy and girl. It appeals to the love of the out-of-doors and to the love of adventure. It portrays the Indian (both good and bad), the soldier, and the scout.

In Uncas and his father we see the Indian at his best, with his wisdom and the too-frequently-forgotten kindness and loyalty which tempered, although they did not eradicate, the more primitive traits of character. In Sly Fox we see the Indian at his worst, with selfishness and cruelty superseding the finer traits. Hawkeye, the scout, is as romantic as he is keen and active, and Munro and Heyward typify the straightforward and fearless soldier.

In the present edition, the editors have tried to put Cooper's narrative into a form which the junior and senior high school pupils of today can enjoy. Lengthy descriptions have been abridged; conversations have been put into terms less formal than in the original; sentence structure and concepts have been simplified. The vocabulary load is lighter than that

◇◇

in many fourth-grade readers, since ninety-five per cent of the words are from the first thousand in Thorndike's *A Teacher's Word Book* and Gates' *Reading Vocabulary for the Primary Grades*.

At the same time the original has been followed as closely as the interests of the modern reader seem to warrant, and it is earnestly hoped that this book will bring pleasure to pupils who would otherwise be denied a most interesting tale.

Other books in this series which provide easy reading material that gives students a chance to feel successful, regardless of their proficiency in reading are: *Around the World in Eighty Days, Captains Courageous, David Copperfield, Eight Treasured Stories, Famous Mysteries, Huckleberry Finn, Lorna Doone, Moby Dick, Robinson Crusoe, Silas Marner, Six Great Stories, Treasure Island, 20,000 Leagues Under the Sea, When Washington Danced,* and *The Years Between.*

The following books have also been specially prepared with a high interest level to appeal to boys and girls with minimum reading skills: *The Boxcar Children, The Flying Trunk, Hidden Silver, 1001 Nights, Six Robbens, Surprise Island,* and *The Yellow House Mystery.*